Also by the Author

Novels

SHADOW OF THE PAST

Stories

THE WINSTON & CHURCHILL CASE FILES
Never Let Go
A Love Supreme
Heart of Suffering
An Equal Sharing of Miseries
A Shadow Upon the Scenes
A Wolf in Wolf's Clothing
Injuries of the Past
A Bodyguard of Lies

Collections

Summer of Sins
Fall of Shadows
Dead of Winter *(coming soon)*

Donnie, Look for Dead of Winter in 2019!

THE SECOND WINSTON & CHURCHILL COLLECTION

FALL OF SHADOWS

DotD Atlanta '18

THACHER E. CLEVELAND

FIRST PRINT EDITION

ISBN: 978-1724924407

For my Mom

Table of Contents

A Shadow
Upon the Scenes

September

"You can't be serious," Lexie Winston said with her feet up on her desk, glaring at her partner.

"Have you ever known me not to be?" Henry Churchill said, standing across from her and leaning against a file cabinet.

She crossed her arms. "You're right, I haven't. But as weird as that is, it doesn't address the question at hand: why do we need to hire another person, let alone him?"

"I'm not talking about hiring another investigator. Just some office help that can keep us organized. Handle billing, do research and make sure our files are organized. This way we can spend more time working on cases," he said, ticking off points on his fingers.

She rolled her eyes. "I hate it when you're reasonable.

But why him?"

Henry sighed, took his suit jacket off and hung it on the coat rack next to the door. "The work that we do ends up being fairly . . . specialized--"

"Because of the spookiness," Lexie interrupted.

Henry nodded. "Yes, because of the spookiness. It makes it a little difficult for us to just run an ad in the paper and hope we get someone who's okay with it. This way we have someone who's had experience with these kinds of things and is prepared for it."

"But him?" she said, taking her feet down and leaning forward. "This guy has some sort of freak-out and turns himself into a monster, and we're supposed to just give him keys to the front door? He's kind of a major weirdo and I'm not entirely sure he's trustworthy. Or sane."

From the small couch in the office about five feet from Lexie's desk, Martin Green cleared his throat. "I'm also right here, so if you want me to wait outside or something that's cool."

Lexie turned to him. "Nah, I'm good. I mean, are you denying that you stalked your ex-girlfriend and turned yourself into a demonic monkey-man bent on rending her limb from limb? Are those facts in dispute?"

Martin opened his mouth to say something, closed it and then just said "Not really, but--"

"Cool," Lexie continued, turning back to Henry. "So

you see my reservations here, right? I mean, this kid isn't exactly the model picture of trustworthiness."

"Martin made some mistakes and we've talked about them," Henry said. "He's very sorry for what he's done and he wants to find a way to turn his experience into a positive one."

"Fantastic," Lexie said. "Why does he have to do it here?"

"We need the help," Henry said.

"Do we need it this bad?"

"I can just wait outside," Martin said, starting to get to his feet. "I mean if you want some privacy or something."

"No, we're fine," Lexie smiled at him

Henry waved for Martin to sit down and he did with a sigh. "It's like dealing with my parents," he muttered.

"Henry, what's to stop him from digging his hands into some other magical . . . thing we come across and making us have to track him down all around the city before he tries to kill someone? Again."

"Okay look," Martin said. "I realize that what I did was stupid--"

"And dangerous," Lexie interrupted.

"And dangerous, but--"

"And irresponsible."

"And irresponsible, but--"

"And gross."

"Gross? What? Come on!"

"You killed a cat and did a weird little cat-blood finger-painting," Lexie said, wiggling her fingers at him. "That's pretty gross, Marty."

"That cat was a dead when I found it. And please don't call me Marty."

"Whatever you say, Marty."

"That's it," he said, getting to his feet and walking out the door. "I was trying to help out but I'd rather get a job at Starbucks than deal with this shit. You figure this thing out on your own."

"Martin, wait," Henry said, glaring at Lexie before following him.

"Oh come on," she said, rolling her eyes and following the two of them. "Don't be so dramatic."

Martin walked through the small reception area outside of Henry and Lexie's office but had stopped at the door leading out into the hallway at Henry's insistence.

"Look, I get it," Martin said, glaring at Lexie standing at the door to the inner office. "I fucked up big time and put everyone in danger, but that's not the kind of thing I'd ever do again. I don't remember much of what happened when I turned into that . . . thing, but there are bits that I do and sometimes it wakes me up in the middle of the night. I would never, ever, let something like that happen again. If what Henry said is true and whoever gave me that book is still out there giving other people stuff like that- then I want to stop them."

"So you remember who it was?" Lexie said.

Martin looked over at Henry and then back at her. "No. Everything about how I got it is a complete blank."

"I think he may have had some sort of spell on him to make him forget," Henry said. "There are things that I can do that could break through that spell, but I'd like to explore some other avenues first."

"So while we wait, why don't we pay him money we could be putting back in the business, right?" she said.

"You know I'm right about this," Henry said. "Martin is genuinely sorry and we definitely need the help."

"Fine," Lexie said lifting her hands in surrender. "But at the first sign of him being creepy I'm going to taser the ever living shit out of him." She turned and walked back into the office.

"See?" Henry said, patting Martin on the shoulder. "I knew she'd come around."

"I'm going to need her to define 'creepy' for me. I really, really don't want to get tased."

"Is this necessary?" Martin said, holding up a bunch of bananas that looked to be just on the other side of ripe.

Lexie shrugged her shoulders. "I thought you might want a snack. Eat some bananas, they're good for you."

"I know they're good for me!" Martin yelled, waving them in the air. "They're full of potassium! But why do you keep leaving them around my desk?"

"Monkeys like bananas," Lexie said.

"I'm not a monkey!" he yelled, waving the bananas so vigorously one of them dropped to the ground at his feet. Henry, who had just walked in to the office, was standing behind Martin in the doorway of the office and let out a deep sigh. Lexie bit her lip as she tried not to grin. Martin turned around and held the bananas out for Henry to see.

"Every day, there's some kind of a banana! Stickers, drawings and now fruit. Real fruit! These were hidden in my desk drawer!" Henry waved the fruit down from his face and stepped around him, hanging his suit jacket on the rack by his desk.

"Really?" Henry said, turning around to look at the still grinning Lexie. "I have two teenagers at home, why do you think I need this at my job?"

"I think of it as contributing to our employee's health plan," she said, failing to maintain a straight face.

"I didn't start working here so I could be harassed!" Martin said. "I wanted to help out, not be picked on."

"No one's picking on you," she said, amusement turning to exasperation.

"This!" Martin said, waving the bunch of bananas again. "This is the definition of picking on!"

"Oh relax," she said, turning back to her computer. "I'm just having a little fun."

"Do I look like I'm having fun? Henry, can you--"

"Henry, look--" she said, the both of them turning to him and trying to talk over each other.

"Stop! Stop!" Henry said, putting his hands up. "Martin, relax. Lexie, stop it with the monkey jokes."

"Thank you," Martin said, tossing the bunch on the table in front of the couch.

"Fine," Lexie said with a touch of annoyance. "How'd last night go?"

"Pretty much the same as in here," Henry said. "Which is disappointing, seeing as how it was a mental hospital."

"So no luck then?" she asked.

Henry shook his head and then motioned for Martin to have a seat on the office couch. "Last night I went to Bellevue to visit with a former client of ours. One who I think had a run-in with the same person that you did."

Martin nodded. "The one who sold me the book."

"Right," Henry said. "We didn't get much of a chance to talk to Mimi Chalmers before--"

"What with her being arrested for murder and all," Lexie said.

"But," Henry continued, glaring at her before turning back to Martin "she's been transferred to a psychiatric hospital now that she's been found mentally unfit to stand trial. I figured I'd try and talk to her to see if she remembers anything about the person that she got her book from, since it seems like it came from the same library as the one you were sold."

"Any luck?" Martin asked. As it had before in the couple of weeks that he'd worked for them, discussing the specifics of the investigation sent a visible ripple of anxiety through him.

Henry shook his head.

"Crap," Lexie said. After doing some digging they had found a couple of incidents that seemed to fit the profile of this mysterious trafficker in the occult. In Massapequa last March, a man was found with his throat ripped out and surrounded by ritualistic items, including a child's coffin and a small book from the same collection as Martin and Mimi's. In January on Staten Island, a family's house was burned to the ground and no trace of the residents were found, living or dead. According to witnesses the fire started suddenly, consuming only the house before dying out on its own. The only thing that was recovered from the scene was an intricate metal box. At first they didn't think there was any connection to the three books, but Henry had had discovered a reference to it in the one they'd found at Martin's apartment.

"So now what?" Martin asked.

"Like I said, there are some things I can do that can possibly break through your memory block. I'd held off going further with it as it could make you a little uncomfortable but after this . . . "

Martin nodded quickly, squeezing both of his hands

together. "I get it. It's not going to hurt is it?"

Henry stood up and walked over to one of the old recliners facing the couch Martin was sitting in. "Normally I'd say no but if this person found a way to put some sort of block on your memories, they may have done something else."

"Christ," Lexie said with annoyance. "What made him so special? He was the only one that they went to all this trouble with."

"Is that true?" Martin asked. "They didn't do something to that other lady?"

Henry shook his head. "I doubt it. She wasn't exactly coherent so it's hard to say but it doesn't seem like it. Then again, given her mental state they may have figured she wasn't going to say anything."

"Okay, okay," Martin said, nodding and staring past Henry. "I'll do it. I don't want anyone else getting hurt if we can stop this."

"Alright. Lock up the front and we'll get started." Henry said, getting up and heading back to his desk.

As Martin stood up he took a deep breath. Before he could head out into the reception area Lexie waved him over to her desk. "All joking aside, this is a good thing you're doing."

Martin nodded, but it seemed like he was trying to convince himself of that more than agreeing with her. "I hope so," he said. "I just hope he doesn't melt my brain or whatever."

Lexie gave a little smile. "Henry knows what he's

doing. The chances of him brain-melting you are pretty slim."

Martin smiled back a little and then turned to leave.

"Hold on," Lexie said. "Before all this goes down there's something important you need to do first?"

"What?" he asked.

"Get rid of those bananas, okay? I think they're going bad."

His smile dropped and he walked off, pausing to snatch the bunch up from the couch. "Don't forget the one on the ground!" she called after him.

"Relaxed?" Henry asked Martin, who was leaning back into one of the recliners facing the couch. He closed his eyes, took a deep breath, opened them again and nodded.

Henry, who was sitting on the couch facing him, reached into his pocket and held up a large silver coin. "Keep an eye on this and try to relax." Martin nodded, eyes already locked onto the coin as it caught the late afternoon light coming in from the window. Lexie watched as Henry rolled the coin back and forth over his knuckles, flipping it end over end and then back again.

"Just listen to my voice Martin," Henry said. "Just listen and relax." It took a second for Lexie to realize she was staring at the coin as well. The edges of her vision were beginning fade to gray and she could feel herself beginning to slide off the edge of her desk that she'd been leaning on. She closed her eyes and shook her head to clear the cobwebs out of her brain.

She stood up straight and opened her eyes just in time to see Martin's flutter and then close. After one more trip across his hand Henry palmed the coin and put it back into his pocket.

"Now what?" she asked.

"In this relaxed state I can take a look inside his head and see if there's something he remembers about how he got the book."

"So what if our mysterious salesperson has in fact been keeping tabs on us and does something about it?"

"Well," Henry said, pulling the coffee table from between the couch and chair the unconscious Martin sat in. "If he or she has then they haven't been having any luck lately. This office has been shielded from most forms of scrying."

"Scrying?" she asked.

"Magical remote viewing. I think whoever is doing this probably has an amateur set of magical skills, seeing as how any serious practitioner wouldn't be selling off items so recklessly. They may know some tricks here and there, but I doubt they'd be able to do anything complex. Help me move the couch."

She stared for a moment and then got up and helped Henry push the sofa into the corner of the room while humming to herself.

"What song is that?" Henry asked.

"Scrying eyes are watching you, they see your every

move," she sang.

"Cute," he said, going in the walk-in storage closet next to his desk. "But in the event that I'm wrong--"

"Stranger things have happened," she interrupted.

"In that case, I'm going to set up a protective circle just to keep anything bad that may happen from escaping," disappearing into the closet.

"I'm becoming less comfortable with this plan."

"Everything will be under control," he said over the sounds of cabinet drawers opening and closing. "Or they will be if I can find the chalk that was in here. Did you move it?"

"I don't think so. Well, maybe a I did. There was a bag of stuff in there that I pushed towards the back to make room for some of the new ammo I picked up the other day."

Henry heaved a sigh she could hear over the sound of charms, boxes and bags being shuffled around in the cabinet. "I realize that it looks chaotic in here but there is a place for everything. Has been for quite some time."

"Are you sure? Because it just looks like piles. Piles older than the hills."

Henry emerged from the room holding a small velvet bag. "Yes, but organized piles. There's a place for ammo on the shelf towards the back."

"I just figured we'd want it closer to the front in case it was really needed. Unlike your magic chalk," she said, sitting on the edge of her desk as she watched him move the second chair to face Martin. He then took the chalk out of the bag and began to draw a circle around the two. When Henry was done he drew a second circle about six inches around the first and then began to draw symbols in the spaces between the two.

"You're mad about the chalk, aren't you?" she said after a few minutes.

"No, I'm not mad about the chalk," he said, not looking up.

"You sound mad."

"I'm really not."

"Really? Because now I'm detecting a tone."

Henry stopped drawing and looked up at her. "No, I'm not mad about the chalk. I'm getting mad that you keep asking me if I'm mad."

"Fine, Fine. Don't get all pissy," she said, putting up a hand and walking around as much of the double circle Henry had drawn as she could. It stretched nearly from the entrance of the small office to the far wall. "For someone drawing on crappy carpet in chalk, this is a pretty decent circle."

"Well it has to be. Believe me, I've had a lot of practice." Henry said, putting the finishing touches on the last symbol and getting to his feet with a grunt of pain.

"So what should I expect if this whole thing goes well?"

"If it goes smoothly then it'll be over pretty quickly. We'll both wake up after a few minutes and I'll either have what we need or I won't, but at least we'll know we tried."

"And if something bad happens?"

"I guess that depends on how bad it is. I'll either be able to handle it or . . . I won't."

"The only thing that's keeping me from getting really worried about this is the idea that the more we talk about it the less likely it is to happen."

Henry chuckled. "If only that were true."

"Allow me my delusions, okay? If something does go wrong what should I do?"

Henry dropped the chalk back into the small velvet bag and walked back to the storage room. After some rattling around, he reemerged. He handed Lexie a card and then stepped into the circle, taking a seat on the edge of the coffee table in front of Martin. "That's Don Porter's number. If something does happen that you don't think you can handle then give him a call. If things go south then whoever's behind this may have a bit more skill and connection than I give them credit for, which means they may run in the same circles I do. Don's one of the only people that I trust to not be a part of anything like that. At the very least, he can point you in the right direction."

"And I take it you don't want me to call Monica?"

"My wife knows the risks involved in this, but I don't want her involved. If something dangerous happens then let her know. Other than that keep her out of it," Henry said, rolling up his sleeves and loosening his tie and shirt collar.

"If you say so," Lexie muttered, walking back to her desk and tossing the card onto it. She walked around to one of the drawers, opened it and placed her holster with the Walther in it on her desk as well as the small video camera they used for surveillance.

"I don't think you'll need that," Henry said, nodding towards the pistol.

"Hey, you have protection rituals and I have mine. Do what you've gotta do, I'll watch your back," she said, setting the camera on top of a pile of papers and pointing it at Martin.

"And that?" Henry asked.

"Well, if any of you starts talking in your sleep at least I'll have some blackmail material. Or we'll be able to go back over this later to make sure we don't miss anything. Either one."

"If it works, there won't be anything to see."

Lexie looked back over at Henry. "And if it doesn't I want evidence of what happened. Because no one will believe me." The camera gave an electronic beep as she started recording.

"Fair enough," Henry nodded. He sat down and placed a hand on Martin's knee, closing his eyes. He sat silently for a moment and then his mouth began to move. After a few moments of silent chanting, both Henry and Martin's bodies shuddered and then fell still, Henry's head lolling to the side limply. Lexie watched for any sign of movement for almost a full minute before she allowed herself to relax.

"Okay," she said to herself, "You got yourself all worried over nothing."

Just as she finished Henry's head snapped up and he stared up at the ceiling. His eyelids fluttered and then he opened his mouth as wide as it could go. She could hear the creak of his jaw straining to open wider and then a pale green mist seeped out of his mouth and nose.

"Ahhhh shit," Lexie said. She reached out and took the Walther from its holster, resting it against her leg.

The mist hovered just above Henry's open mouth before being sucked back in like cigarette smoke. Henry closed his mouth and turned his head to look at Lexie, his eyes open but covered with a pale, green film.

"Well," he said in a voice that wasn't his own, "I wouldn't say you were worried for nothing."

"This is weird," Martin said, looking around. He and Henry were standing in Martin's old apartment and sitting in the corner on the computer was Martin, clicking away and oblivious to the other version of himself across the room.

"This is your memory," Henry said, walking around. "Probably the first time whoever sold you the book contacted you. Does anything seem familiar?"

Martin walked around, peering at the various piles of things laying around the room. "Well, I'm sitting and doing stuff on the computer so this could be any time since I moved out of here to when I was nine."

"Anything helpful?"

Martin squatted down, looking at a stack of comic books on the floor next to his bed. "Okay, well judging from these comics it's about six months ago. Somewhere around there."

"You're sure?"

Martin reached down to move a comic but his hand passed right through it. "Wow, that's . . . weird. But yeah, pretty sure. I try to keep the most recent ones on top of the pile. So now what?" he asked, getting to his feet and looking around.

"We wait and see what happens," Henry said, walking over to the memory-phantom Martin and looking over his shoulder. "This is . . . interesting. You're writing about your breakup on some website."

"Yeah, yeah," Martin said, hurrying over to Henry's side. "It's just self-indulgent whiny break-up crap. I don't even know why I put it on my blog I just wanted to get it out there for some reason. I'm sure it's super-boring and super-embarrassing."

Henry nodded and walked away. "I guess you did that a lot, huh?"

"Yeah, pretty much. Especially after Helen and I broke up. And a lot of the time while we were living together."

"Huh," Henry said.

"Yeah, yeah," Martin said, leaning over his own shoulder to read what he was typing. "Well I remember making this post but I don't really remember anything weird happening while I was doing it." He looked from the screen to the memory of himself. "Is that what I look like?" he asked, looking down at himself. "Jesus, I gotta get to a gym or something."

"You've looked much worse," Henry said.

"Thanks, I think. I'm embarrassed seeing myself all worked up like this. When I think about our relationship now, I realize that it never would've worked in a million years."

"Sometimes when you're so wrapped up in something you can't see it clearly. If it makes you feel any better, you seem a lot more together than when we first met."

"Well like you said, you've seen me at much worse." There was a tone from the computer and Martin looked back at the screen. "Hold on, this is new."

"What is it?" Henry said, walking over to join him.

"It's an instant message," Martin said. "Which is weird because I don't really like using instant messaging. This I would've remembered."

"Then now we're getting somewhere," Henry said.

Hey there. I read your blog and I just wanted to say I know how you feel. I've had a few bad breakups too, the message read.

After staring at it in confusion for a moment the past-Martin typed a reply. Who is this? How'd you get my

29

messenger handle?

I'm good with computers, it replied.

Past-Martin still looked confused but kept typing. Well thanks for being extra creepy then. Good luck in your future endeavors.

I know, this seems weird but after reading about what that chick put you through I think I know a way for you to get back at her.

Martin's brow furrowed in thought and then after a few moments he typed Why do you think I want to get back at her?

She broke your heart, Martin. Isn't that reason enough?

I'm sad but I'm not crazy, Martin replied. Kindly go away.

Fair enough, was the reply a few moments later. But if you change your mind come and see me at The Lodge on Astoria. I'm there most weeknights and I'm willing to bet you don't have anything better to do. The least I can do is buy you a drink to help ease your troubles.

Martin shook his head. Thanks, but I'll take a rain check on your offer to roofie and axe murder me. Fuck off somewhere else now, kthnxbai. With an annoyed click of his mouse he closed the chat window.

"Okay, that's weird," Martin said, standing up straight. "I really think I'd have remembered that."

"Well that's the whole point of this, isn't it?" Henry asked, not taking his eyes off the memory-version of Martin. "See? Look."

Martin turned around just in time to see his past self let his head sag to the side as his eyes fluttered shut for a

30

second. He almost slid out of his chair but quickly righted himself with a start. After a few seconds of looking around in confusion he continued typing.

"That was it? What was that?" Martin asked.

"There was probably a charm on the message to make you forget it on the conscious level. A part of your mind remembers it, and I'm willing to bet a couple of nights from now you get the urge to go to The Lodge."

"No way," Martin said. "I can't possibly be that stupid."

Before he finished talking his bedroom swirled around the two of them like someone erasing an etch-a-sketch. When everything settled back into place Martin's room was replaced by a dimly lit and nearly empty rustic-looking bar. Above the back of the bar, carved in wood above a mirror and rows of alcoholic beverages was a sign that read "The Lodge." There was the creak of a door opening and both Henry and Martin turned to see another past-Martin walk in the front door, cautiously taking in the place.

"You were saying?" Henry said.

"Jesus," Martin said, watching himself walk across the room to an empty spot at the bar near the back. "Just when I think I can't get any dumber. Now what?"

"Now we wait," Henry said, walking back to where past-Martin was sitting. "I'm sure whoever sent that message will be along shortly."

"Um, Henry? I think they're already here," Martin said,

31

tugging on Henry's sleeve and pointing to the other side of the room. Henry turned and saw a figure making its way to past-Martin. It took Henry a second to realize that it had no distinguishing features and was nothing more than a blurred out humanoid shape just a little bit taller than he was. Henry blinked to try to clear his vision, but no matter what he did the person who sat at the empty stool next to past-Martin remained featureless. He couldn't even make out the color and style of their clothes, let alone if it was male or female.

"You're seeing that too, right?"

"I am," Henry said, stepping closer while moving Martin behind him.

"This is bad, right?"

"It isn't good," Henry said.

The blur walked over to where past-Martin was sitting and took the seat next to him. Martin looked up for a moment and even through the blur they got the distinct impression that it was smiling. "Is this seat taken?" it asked, in a nondescript voice that sounded like it was coming off of a damaged audio tape.

"No, go ahead," Martin said, glancing over and then flagging down the bartender to order a beer. The blur did the same.

"What does this mean?" Martin said, leaning in to whisper in Henry's ear.

"You don't have to whisper," Henry said, not taking his

eyes off the interaction at the bar. "It means that whoever did this is a bit more skilled than I thought."

"That sounds bad."

"No, I just underestimated them. That's fine. At least we can watch what happened and then maybe I can break through whatever block they've put around themselves."

He walked a little closer, squinting at the blur who was now just sitting in silence next to an equal silent Martin, the two just drinking their beers. After a couple of moments the blur turned and looked at Martin. "So are you feeling any better?" it asked him.

"What?" he said, confused.

"It's been a couple of days since you posted anything on your blog and I was just wondering if you're still all heartbroken."

"How do you know who I am?"

The blur reached over and touched Martin's arm before he could pull away. "I messaged you the other day, asking if you were interested in finding a way to get back at her."

Martin pulled away, confusion on his face. "What are you . . . oh man, yeah. That message I got. How did I forget about that?"

The blur gave a little chuckle. "Well, I had a little hand in that. But the important thing is that you're here and we can chat face to face."

"Why would I do that? I don't even know who you are."

"I'm--" the blur said, extending its hand for a handshake and then stopping in mid-sentence. It took a second for Henry to realize that not only did the blur stop but everything else in the bar had stopped as well. Even the drinks being poured by the bartender had stopped in mid-flow.

"What's going on?" Martin said, looking around as panic crept into his voice.

"I don't know," Henry said. walking around and taking a quick look at everything. "Do you feel okay?"

"Yeah," Martin said. "Aside from rising panic and terror, I don't feel particularly bad."

"Well that'll change," the rubbed-out sounding voice of the blur said.

Henry and Martin turned as the blur got out of its seat and began to walk towards them. "I'm really kind of surprised that you went this route, Mr. Churchill. Then again I expected you to not just be incapable of letting this go but to underestimate me as well."

"Who are you?" Henry said, stepping closer to block its path to Martin.

"Telling you would kind of defeat the purpose of all this, you think?" it said, waving its hands over the blurry and indistinct form.

"Why did you stop this memory? What are you trying

to keep us from seeing?"

"Honestly? I stopped it because it's boring as crap. No offense Martin, but once I get you calmed down and loosened up with a few drinks you spent a lot of time droning on about your ex and your relationship and what you'd change and all that jazz. I think it's a good three hours before I get you to accept my offer and buy the book. Besides if I kept going you'd hear my name and again," another wave of indistinct hands, "defeats the purpose. The question before us now is what I'm going to do with the two of you."

"Who are you?" Lexie asked, getting up from the edge of the desk and walking towards the boundary of the circle.

"You guys are really hung up on that, aren't you?" Henry's body said in scratchy, rubbed out version of Henry's voice. "Here's a question for you: why do you two give a shit?"

"People are getting hurt," Lexie said. "You're tricking them into buying things they don't understand that are dangerous."

"So what, when you're done with me you're going to go after every gun shop in the tri-state area?"

"That's different," Lexie said. She was as close to the edge of the circle as she dared without looking down and checking to make sure her feet weren't stepping into it.

"Oh really? How?" Henry's body took a step forward and then jerked back, like there was a cord wrapped around his waist holding him back. Henry looked down at the circle on the floor and then up at Lexie with a wide smile. The smile bothered her worse than the green film covering his irises.

"That clever bastard. I knew he'd try something like this and I'd have to give him a poke to get the two of you to leave me alone but I figured he'd underestimate me."

"Looks like you were wrong. I guess you don't know him as well as you think."

"True, true," Henry said, kneeling down to get a closer look at the runes. "Oh these are good. I'm going to have to ask him where he got them from. People love shit with runes. Gives a real sense of authenticity, y'know?"

"No, not really. So what's the play here, body snatcher? You said you wanted us to leave you alone but I can tell you that's not going to happen. Just deliver whatever lame-ass threat you've got and we'll get right back on your trail."

"Sure, sure," the body snatcher said, getting back to his feet but grimacing in pain and surprise as weight was put on Henry's bad knee. "Jesus. He needs to take better care of himself," he said, patting Henry's protruding belly.

"How 'bout you let him out and I'll let him know," Lexie said.

"You'd like that, wouldn't you? Then again, with me in here I could tell you all kinds of things you don't know about Harlem's oldest monster hunter. Speaking of, did he ever tell you how he hurt his knee?"

Lexie opened her mouth to say something but the body snatcher held up a finger. "Ah ah, I know for a fact that he didn't. Just like I know that you two have known each other for almost a year and you really don't know that much about him, do you?"

"Look," Lexie said. "This is cute and all, but we've got stuff to do. Make your point and let us getting on with hunting your ass down."

Henry smiled. It was still unnerving. "I like you. You're sassy. But here's the point. Leave this alone, okay? The only people who are getting hurt are the people who are stupid enough to try a quick fix for their problems."

"And if we don't you'll what? Be loud and annoying while trapped in a circle?"

"You don't seem that concerned that I'm in here with these two and can do pretty much whatever I want."

"Not really," Lexie said. "Because if you'd wanted them dead they'd be dead. You just think you're going to put a scare into us and we'll just give this whole thing up. If you think you know us so well, I figure that you'd know we're not going to just roll over on this. So really you're just wasting our time."

The body snatcher shrugged Henry's shoulders and began walking the perimeter of the circle, putting his hands in his pockets. "Okay, okay. I get it, you're not going to scare that easily. After all you're one bad ass chick who's seen it all, right? Before fighting monsters and demons and nasty folks like me you were a cop and a soldier and just rough and tumble right down to the core."

"Something like that."

"Cool, cool," he said, stopping behind the chair with Martin's still slumbering body in it. "Since you're so cool, this probably won't bother you that much, huh?" He leaned forward, putting his hands on Martin's shoulders. Martin's face winced for a moment and then he began to shake, at first just like he was having a bad dream but after a few moments it turned into a full blown violent seizure.

"Still think I'm bluffing?"

"I don't like this," Martin said, backing away from the two of them. "Can't we just clap our hands and wake up or something?"

"You could try," the blur said. "but I don't think you will. Or more specifically I don't think he'll let you."

"What the hell does that mean?" Martin asked, his voice shaking.

"It means he's too curious to find out about me," the blur said, walking around Henry. "He's wondering how someone he thought was just some dumb-ass amateur pulled off a trick like this, am I right?"

"I'm a little curious," Henry said, moving to keep himself between Martin and the blur.

"Oh come on! Don't play all calm, cool and collected

with me, man! You've gone to a lot of trouble to track down little 'ol me, even exposing your boy friday to some serious danger just at the chance you'd catch a glimpse at me. Ballsy, man. I like it."

"What does . . . it mean, serious danger? You said this would be harmless," Martin said, stepping up behind Henry, who put an arm out to keep Martin back but didn't take his eyes off the blur in front of him.

"If I was some rube selling knick-knacks on eBay then yeah, this would've been a walk in the park. But he just figured that because I was in need of cash and was smart enough to use what I've got that I must also be stupid. Frankly, Henry, I'm a little hurt."

"Do we know each other?" Henry said.

"That'd be telling, wouldn't it? And by the way, nice touch with the protection circle. I knew you'd give this a try and figured I'd be able to give you and GI Jane up there a wake up call, but it looks like that's not in the cards, is it?"

Henry closed his hand into a fist. "Is that bad?" Martin asked, sensing the rise in anger. "Can someone just tell me what's going on?"

"It's simple," the blur said, pacing in a circle around them. "I put a little trap on this memory of yours so that when Mr. Churchill here started digging around for it I'd get the heads up, so to speak and voila, here I am. Now what I hadn't counted on was the particular protection circle he used on the off chance I'd try a trick like this. What is that anyway, Akkadian? Enochian? That's the good shit, let me tell you. So here's the pickle: I popped into this shared little magical mind-meld you two were having and figured I'd create a little anarchy. Unfortunately there's not much I can do trapped in the circle and even more unfortunately I can't leave."

"Why not?" Martin asked.

"Because magic has rules and most of them are really fucking annoying. In this case it's like building a ship in a bottle. Once the ship is built you can't get it out without smashing the bottle or tearing the ship apart."

"Which one am I?" Martin said, and Henry could feel him begin to shiver.

"I wouldn't be too thrilled to be either one of them if I were you. And if anyone should be worried it's old Henry here. He's the one who sprung the trap so it's his body I'm taking for a ride at the moment. By the way, lay off the hot dogs. Maybe do a little pilates or something. This thing is like driving a station wagon loaded down with bricks."

"Get to the point," Henry said through gritted teeth.

"Oh, you're pissed huh? Look, it's real simple. I ran it past the lady upstairs and she doesn't seem to get it but I'm willing to bet that you do. Back. Off. All I'm doing is selling stuff I don't need to people dumb enough to think they can shortcut their way through life. I'm the living embodiment of the American dream, okay?"

"And if I say no?" Henry said.

"'If you say no?' Ha, listen to yourself. Of course you're going to say no. So what I'm going to have to do is hurt one of you."

"Oh Jesus," Martin said.

"Yeah, you better be scared. Because hurting Mr. Churchill, who has been waiting his whole life for a noble death isn't going to mean much. But you . . . poor, heartbroken Martin. You're going to have to be what I use to make my point."

"Leave him alone," Henry said, holding a hand out between them and the blur.

"That's cute that you think you can just Gandalf me but you're forgetting that this is his mind we're in." A tremor ran through the floor they were standing on. "It's not like I have to touch him to . . . well, touch him."

Behind Henry, Martin made a sudden choking sound and dropped to the ground. Henry turned to see him writhing in pain, body flailing wildly. "Hold on," Henry said, trying to hold Martin still.

"Are you still not getting the concept here?" The blur said, stepping closer. "This isn't real, it's projection. What I'm doing to him doesn't have any physical source. You can't just keep him from biting his tongue and hope he makes it through. I'm burning him from the inside and there's nothing you can do to stop it."

Henry placed his hands on Martin's chest, pressing him down to the floor and leaving only his arms and legs kicking and flailing on the ground. He closed his eyes and began to whisper to himself.

"What are you doing?" the blur said, coming closer.

He looked up at it, blood seeping from his eyes and running down his face. "Now who's underestimating who?"

"Stop it," Lexie said, stepping closer to the circle. "Leave him alone."

"Why?" the body snatcher said, shrugging Henry's shoulders. "You don't even like him."

"Just because he's a dorky idiot doesn't mean I want him dead. Especially by your hands."

"Well, well, look who's trying to play hero all of the sudden."

"I'm not playing," Lexie said, walking back over to her desk and taking the Walther from its holster and aiming it at Henry.

"Great plan, Lexie. You going to shoot your partner? Like you shot Henry's last partner?"

"I can shoot him without killing him and I bet you'll feel some of it."

"Why are you doing this?"

"Because you're pissing me off."

"No, not the gun. I have a theory about that already,

but why are you down here in the city playing hero? Do you really give a shit about saving people or do you just have nothing better to do?"

"A little from column a, a little from column b."

"So goddamn flippant. Is this really the life you wanted? Trying to protect people who are too stupid to look after themselves while you pick up the pieces of your own mistakes?"

"You talk like you know a whole lot about me," Lexie said, stepping closer. "It's a shame so much of it is bullshit."

"Not me," the body snatcher said, taking a hand off Martin's twitching form to tap a finger against Henry's temple. "Him. While I've got him preoccupied I can do a little surface scan of what he's got running around up here and let me tell you, he thinks about you a lot. You always pester him to tell you more and let you in but the fact of the matter is that he doesn't trust you."

"Bullshit."

"Oh, he trusts you in a 'She's not going to steal my stuff' kind of way, but when it comes to you spending the rest of your life fighting demons, tracking down magical crap, and risking your life for idiots, he has some doubts. One of these days, he figures, you're just going to toss your hands up in the air and go 'Enough.'"

"That'd never happen," Lexie said.

Henry's mouth smiled. "Hey, it was pretty easy for you

to do with your old life. Kept it just shallow enough for you to walk away when the going got tough. No reason you wouldn't do that again here."

"Is that what you think?"

"No, it's what he thinks."

"You're full of shit," Lexie felt an edge creeping into her voice.

"It doesn't sound like your heart is in it anymore," Henry smiled wider. "Maybe you're closer to calling it quits than he thought." Before it could say any more, Martin's body tensed, rising up from the chair for a moment as if he was about to stand, and then dropped back into the chair and lay still.

"What the fuck did you do?" Lexie said, anger now fully focused as she aimed at Henry. A part of her was disturbed at how easy it was now.

"Well, that was interesting," Henry said, and before Lexie could demand a response she noticed Martin's chest rising in slow, even breaths. "See? He's . . . " the body snatcher trailed off and then put a hand to Henry's face. When it took it off Lexie could see blood running down Henry's nose.

"Well that can't be good," the body snatcher said with a wry smile and then shuddering and dropping down to one knee.

"What's happening?" Martin said, his violent spasming stopped.

"Oh you are good," The blur said, stepping back from Henry and Martin.

"Quite the opposite, really," Henry said, wiping the blood that he'd wept off his face and then flinging the excess drops from his hand.

"Now, now, don't--" the blur started, waving a finger before Henry flew at it. He struck the thing square in the chest like he'd been fired from a canon and then drove it to the ground, hands gripping around its throat.

"Do you think this is a fucking game!" Henry yelled as it writhed underneath him. "Do you think there aren't any fucking consequences to what you're playing with?"

"H . . . how?" the blur gasped out.

"You think our projections don't mean anything in here? You think you can't feel pain in here if I inflict it on you?"

"Okay, okay!" the blur yelled. There was something in its voice that was almost human sounding now.

"There you are," Henry snarled. "Now that someone's fighting back you find it hard to keep up your little disguise, huh? Let me take care of that for you." Henry took a hand from the thing's throat and raised it in the air. A noise came from his mouth that may have been some sort of language but sounded to Martin like a guttural growl and the hand burst into flame. Martin sprang up, backing away from the two of them as Henry pressed his flaming hand into the center of the blur's chest. The thing's scream crackled like static and then became all too human, shrill and high pitched.

"Oh fuck," Martin said, getting to his feet.

"What's the matter?" Henry growled down at the blur, leaning in to press his weight against the thing's chest. "Finally getting a taste of what real magic is like?" Martin could see the blurring effect around the person begin to crackle and flicker.

"Henry, whoa man, come on let's just go!" Martin said, trying to make himself heard over the screaming as he inched closer to the slumped over Henry putting all of his weight into the blur's chest.

"No," snarled Henry, his voice deeper and slurred. "This is what we came for. If this piece of shit is going to play with fire then it's going to get burned."

"Come on, man!" Martin said, close enough to tug on his sleeve. "I didn't sign up for torture!"

"Torture?" Henry said, turning to look at Martin. "This is past torture."

"Jesus fuck!" Martin yelled, drawing back. The brown of Henry's skin had faded to a sickly yellow and his eyes had turned a solid deep red, blood weeping from them. Four small horns protruded in an arc across his forehead and when Henry snarled at him his teeth were all narrow and came to long points.

"This is revenge, for you and everyone this bastard has hurt," Henry grinned, his smile spreading wider than it should and revealing more pointed teeth.

"Fuck you," the blur said, raising its hands and sending green electrical sparks into Henry's demonic visage. Henry yelled in pain, easing up enough for the blur to almost push him off. As the sparks shot from the hands, Martin could see some detail- long painted nails and slender fingers adorned with rings.

Henry smacked the hands away with an angry yell and drove the blur back down to the ground with both hands erupting with fire. Henry raised his head and howled along with the renewed high pitched screams and a pair of large leather bat wings tore through his shirt and spread wide.

"Well this isn't going as planned," the body snatcher said, holding on the chair Martin was sleeping in to keep Henry's body upright. Blood was trickling from both of Henry's nostrils in a steady flow.

"What are you doing to him?" Lexie said.

"Well," it said, lowering Henry's body down to the ground with a grunt of pain and then leaning against the back of the chair. "Your buddy still has a few tricks up his sleeve, and if I can't hurt loverboy over here then I'm going to have to make an example of Mr. Churchill."

"Let him go."

"I would if I could," the body snatcher said, it's off-pitch version of Henry's voice cracking. "But this circle here keeps me trapped, so I guess I'm going to have to take my frustrations out on him. What a shame." It held up Henry's hand and coughed a loud, wet cough into that shook Henry's body. "Whoops," it said, holding up Henry's hand to show it spattered with blood. "That can't be good."

"Tell me who you are and I'll let you go," Lexie said.

"Well that's a terrible offer. Why don't I just keep kicking the crap out of your buddy until his spleen gives out or something?"

"Because then where will you go? If his body dies I bet you'll still be trapped in this circle. I wonder how your body will fare in the meantime."

"Are you really that hardcore, Lexie? Let your partner die, let his wife and kids know that you could've saved him by just wiping out one teensy bit of chalk but you just wouldn't?"

"Do you want to find out?"

The body snatcher smiled, showing Henry's blood-stained teeth. "Y'know, you're my kind of girl."

Martin pushed himself all the way back to the bar, scrambling backwards like a terrified crab as he watched Henry-turned-demon roll around on the floor with the blurred out figure, with bits of fire and arcs of lightning sparking passing between them.

The blur effect around the woman was faltering, giving Martin glimpses of what she looked like. Long dark hair, bright red lips. It was just flashes but he could feel the familiarity of it.

Even the bar was beginning to seem more familiar.

"This is not good," Henry's voice said from behind him.

Martin sprung up and turned around. "What the hell, man? What the fuck is going on here?"

"Bad news," Henry, leaning on the bar and watching the two fight. "We need to get out of here before this gets worse."

"Worse?" Martin said, waving an arm at the two fighting across the room. "How could this get worse?"

With a roar the demon picked up the blurred woman and hurled her towards the front of the bar where she crashed into the wall and dropped down to the ground and out of sight. With a snarl it turned its attention to Martin, and when it saw Henry standing next to him it smiled its awful razor-toothed smile and walked towards them

"Jailor," it growled, dragging its claws against the ground.

"I've gotta stop asking that," Martin said, scrambling over the bar.

"It might be a good idea," Henry said, holding up a hand which began to glow uncomfortably bright, eliciting a shriek of pain from the beast approaching them.

"What are we going to do?" Martin said, ducking under the bar.

"We have to break the spell holding us here, which is

up to our friend over there. But even if she wants to, she's still trapped by the protection circle that I made before I went under."

"So we're screwed, is what you're saying."

Henry winced, taking a step back as the light from his palm flickered for a moment. Martin felt the bar shake behind him and heard the demon roar angrily again. "Not entirely," Henry said, "but first things first. If I don't take care of this thing then we are, in fact, screwed."

With a grimace of pain Henry's light intensified and he stepped forward, bracing himself against the bar.

"Give it up," Lexie said, watching Henry's body slide further down to the floor. "You've got no way out. Tell me your name and I'll let you go."

"Oh yeah," the body snatcher chuckled, which turned into a violent cough that spattered flecks of blood on Henry's shirt. "You'll let me go after you verify that I'm telling the truth and possibly only after you swing by my place and ransack it. I'm no dummy."

"So you'd rather let yourself die?"

"Oh no, this is you letting your partner die. Me? I'll be just fine."

"Yeah, you look like fine alright."

"This," the body snatcher waved Henry's finger around the blood on his shirt and lips. "This is just uncomfortable. I can handle this. Your buddy not so much. Seems like he's got a lot going on in here, maybe a little bit more than I had accounted for. That's fine, I can just wait it out. But can he? Well, that's up to you."

"You're bluffing," Lexie said, lowering her gun a bit.

"You wish I was bluffing." More coughing. "Face it, Lexie. The only way out is for you to cut your losses and let me go. Otherwise you're going to lose a whole lot more."

"I don't--" she was interrupted by more violent coughing, which doubled Henry face down onto the ground. Even when the coughing subsided Henry's body continued to shake and twitch. "Enough," Lexie said, trying not to let any of her anxiety show in her voice. "Quit with the dramatics and tell me what I want to know."

The shaking stopped and his body lay there, perfectly still.

"Hey," Lexie said after a few moments. "Knock it off, alright?"

The body remained still but began a low, rumbling moan.

"Look," Lexie started, but stopped when Henry's head rose from the ground. The green tinge in his eyes that had been there was now replaced with red, and tears of blood began to flow down his face.

"Henry?"

Henry's mouth opened as wide as it could and the

moan turned into a growl. His whole body began to shake again.

"Quit it," Lexie said, raising her voice over the long, monotonous rumble. It stopped for a moment and then was replaced a deep, rumbling mixture of chants and growls that hurt Lexie's ears.

"Enough!" she yelled, trying to drown out the sound. "Henry, talk to me! What's going on in there?"

The growl-chant continued and Henry's body crawled forward until it reached the boundaries of the protection circle. The chant picked up a notch, rising in speed and tone as Henry's body shook even more, pressing against the boundary of the magic.

"Henry," Lexie shouted, backing up against her desk without taking her eyes off of him. "If you're in there then you need to let me know, alright? This is light years beyond okay."

Henry sat up, kneeling and leaning forward to press his palms against the barrier. The cacophony pouring out of him rose in volume, his face straining as his mouth opened wide and his eyes nearly bulged from their sockets.

"Fuck this," Lexie said, leaning over her desk and pulling open the center drawer. She rooted around in it, not taking an eye off of Henry as she tried to find what she was looking for by touch. After a few seconds she found it, snatched it out of the drawer and stood up straight. She stepped forward and swept part of the chalk in the protection circle away with her foot. Without the power of the circle to hold him up Henry fell forward, the chanting momentarily muffled as he landed on his face.

There was a break in the chanting and Henry's body shook again. He pushed himself up and turned to look up at her. His eyes were still blood red, his face still stained with blood. His mouth opened and before he could say anything she jabbed the taser into his arm and triggered it, sending about a million volts through him and dropping him to the ground.

"Holy shit," Martin said behind her. She turned quickly and when he saw the taser in one hand and pistol in the other he leapt out of the chair and backed up, hands in the air. "I thought you were kidding about the taser." He paused, looking around the room as if it was the first time he'd been there. "So wait, what the fuck happened?"

***

It was about an hour before Henry said anything, and even when he did it was with a dead flat voice that Lexie was fairly sure he was using to cover his own irritation.

"That could've gone better," he said, flexing the arm Lexie had tased and wincing in pain.

"No shit, really?" she said, hopping down from her desk where she had been perched ever since Henry had regained consciousness.

"I feel like I was hit by a truck," Martin said around a mouthful of banana and tossing the peel into the trash. "That was a pretty excruciating experience for something that wasn't supposed to melt my brain."

"I get it," Henry said. "This did not go as planned. I can assure you I didn't want to be tasered today."

"Was it at least worth it? Up until the end whoever that was that hijacked your body was convinced we still didn't know who they were."

"Who she was," Henry said.

"She? So you saw something?"

"It was just a glimpse. Did you see it?" Henry asked Martin.

"Yeah," he said. "I'm surprised you did. You seemed . . . indisposed."

"What exactly happened to you two in there?" Lexie asked. "Out here it was just Henry walking around and being kind of bitchy. Which now makes a lot more sense."

"I can't even explain it," Martin said, breaking another banana from the bunch and peeling it. "It was like being in a memory but then it wasn't."

"The spell she cast allowed us to see Martin's memories up to a certain point, but she blocked what she looked like. Initially."

"Then what happened?"

Martin looked over at Henry. "It was complicated."

"Complicated? You two took turns thrashing around like a couple of epileptics and then Henry topped it off by bleeding all over himself and talking in tongues."

Henry looked down at his the stains on his shirt. He'd washed the blood off of his face and hands but there were still spatters of it everywhere. "That would explain why I feel so lousy," he said. "But it was mostly a show to try to get us to let her out. The circle trapped her consciousness with ours when we triggered the spell affecting Martin's memories, so her only way out was if the circle was broken."

Lexie shrugged her shoulders. "I'm not sorry. I wasn't about to have some sort demonic stand off while you bled out all over the carpet. The real question is, if you saw her can you recognize her? Are we any closer to finding her?"

Henry looked over at Martin. "Do you remember anything more now? The spell repressing those memories should be broken."

Martin nodded. "It's weird to realize the gaps that I didn't even know I had. But yeah, I remember her. She's a little older than me and said her name was Christine, but I'm pretty sure we can all agree that's probably not true. But I remember what she looks like."

Henry nodded. "Good. Did she say anything out here?"

"Oh yeah," Lexie said. "She knows us, Henry. Well, she knows you. And she knows about what happened to

Owen."

Henry leaned back on the sofa and ran a hand over the thin layer of hair on his head and let out long sigh.

"Am I missing something? Who's Owen?"

"Owen McCabe was my partner here for almost twenty years before Lexie and I started working together."

"And what happened to him?"

"He got shot. A lot. Until he was dead," Lexie said.

"Who shot--" Martin started, until Lexie glared at him. "Oh crap, you shot him didn't you?"

"In my defense," Lexie said, "He was trying to kill us."

Henry got off the couch and walked over to his desk. "What happened to Owen is a perfect example of how dangerous what this girl is doing. Owen had been doing this for a long time and he still got seduced by evil."

"Could she be someone with a grudge? Did she sound pissed off about you killing him?" Martin asked.

Lexie shook her head. "Not really. What happened to him is a matter of public record, so it's not exactly a secret if you know what you're looking for."

"If she's been paying attention to us that makes her that much easier to find. But for now we should probably just go home and rest. It's been a long day."

Martin nodded. "Sure. That sounds like a great plan, even though I'm terrified to close my eyes."

Henry nodded a goodbye and headed into the supply

closet. Lexie waited until Martin gathered his stuff and left before following him in there. On one side of the small room there were shelves built in to the wall, all over flowing with various boxes and papers. In the back there were various piles of more boxes, some of them notes scrawled over them. Henry was scowling at himself in the full length mirror next to the large cabinet opposite the shelves.

"So how bad was it?" she asked.

"Not great. It could've been worse, but whoever she is she's got a lot more talent than I gave her credit for," Henry growled, loosening his tie.

"Now sound mad."

"Now I am mad," he said, opening the one of the cabinet drawers and pulling out another white shirt and pair of khaki pants. "A little bit at myself and a lot more at her. I thought anyone foolish enough to sell dangerous things like this wouldn't have the talent to really know what they were or how to use them but she does. She knows and doesn't seem to care, which is exceptionally dangerous."

"And you're mad that you underestimated her. Do you think there's a connection between her and Owen?"

Henry shook his head. "Owen had a couple of mutual friends but no family that he talked to. He didn't really keep a lot of secrets."

Lexie nodded, realizing she wasn't the first partner that Henry had some dissimilarities with.

"How's the knee?" she asked.

He waved his hand back and forth, leaning up against the cabinet and bending down to untie his shoes. "It's been better."

"She was a little put off by it," Lexie said. "Plus she was concerned about your weight."

Henry scowled. "Yeah, that message was passed along. Anything else?"

"I've got it on tape if you want to check it out. Some pretty wild stuff."

He shook his head. "Smoke and mirrors. You should probably just delete it."

"You think? You don't want to check it out and see if there's anything that might jog your memory or help make a connection?"

"I dealt with her enough in Martin's head. That's all I need. Just delete it."

Lexie watched him kick off his shoes and realized that for the first time she could tell he was hiding something from her. She'd been a cop for years before Owen's shooting and she prided herself on having a pretty good instinct for such a thing. The part that bothered her most was that she couldn't tell if she was noticing it for the first time, or if Henry was so rattled by what had happened that he'd let his guard down. She didn't care for the implication of the latter and even less about the fact that she realized she was letting what the woman in Henry's body had said get to her.

"So you're fine then? All that shaking and coughing and bleeding from the eyes and you're fine?"

Henry sighed, standing up straight again. "Yes. It was nothing and I feel fine. Can I change out of these bloodstained clothes now? I don't want to get arrested on the way home."

"Okay, okay. Say, you never did tell me what happened to your knee."

"No I didn't," Henry said, unbuttoning his shirt. Lexie raised her eyebrows at him. "If you must know, I wrenched it while chasing someone about ten years ago. Almost tore my ACL. Now if you don't mind, a little privacy please."

"Fine," Lexie said, rolling her eyes. "Like you've got anything I want to see."

She walked over to her desk, checked to make sure the drawer where she kept her Walther, taser and other toys was locked and then picked up the camera. After thinking about it for a moment she dropped it in her purse, grabbed that and her coat and headed for the door. "I'm taking off," she called out the Henry. "I'll see you tomorrow." He mumbled a response and she walked out of the office. She waited until she was out of the building and walking towards the MTA stop before she took out her phone and dialed a number.

"Hey, it's Lexie Winston. Good, good. Look, I had a question about something and I was wondering if I could get your take on it. Yeah, it's about Henry. I'm a little worried about him. Nothing too serious, but I wanted to get your opinion on it. I'll send you the video."

When he heard her close the door and walk down the hallway Henry stepped out of the closet in his undershirt and pants, walked through the reception area and locked the door to the office. He headed back into the closet, took off the undershirt and looked at himself in the mirror again. He felt like he'd been beaten with sticks and there were still little patches on his body from where he'd sweated blood. He leaned in close, getting a good look at the tattoo on his chest just above his heart. It was a circle, similar to the one he'd drawn on the floor earlier but some of the symbols were different. In the middle of the circle was a scar in the shape of symbol unlike the others. Angular, jagged and weathered with age. Henry ran his fingers around the tattooed circle, which had been touched up four years ago when it had begun to fade. When he could see no flaw or break in it he let out a long breath of relief.

"Not today," he said to himself in the mirror. "Not today and never again."

A Wolf in Wolf's Clothing

October

"Hey Martin?" Lexie yelled into the reception area outside the office without looking up from her phone. "Is 'maced' a word?"

"I think so," an unfamiliar woman's voice said. "Like, 'That guy was asking for it, so I maced him.'"

Lexie, who had been leaning back in her chair with her feet on her desk, snapped her head up so fast she almost fell over. A woman that looked to be Lexie's age stood in the doorway, thumbs hooked into the pockets of her jeans. She was just over five feet tall with shoulder length auburn hair and wore a light leather jacket and a messenger bag slung over her shoulder. Ever since getting a job as a private investigator, Lexie wondered if she'd ever encounter the stereotypical "sultry dame" walking in with a problem only she could solve and now here she was.

"That sounds about right," Lexie said, taking her feet off the desk and setting her phone down.

"Sorry to just walk in but there wasn't anyone at the desk," she said, nodding at the empty reception area behind her. As if on cue, Martin walked in from the hallway and froze in place when he realized the two women were staring at him.

"Well there he is now," Lexie said. "Good job with the receptioning there, champ."

"Sorry," he said. "I said I was going to the bathroom but you were preoccupied with the game on your phone. And all your professionalism."

"Anyway," their visitor said, "I'm looking for Owen McCabe. Is he here?"

Lexie leaned forward. "No, he's not. Can I ask who you are?"

"My name's Harmony. He was a friend of my dad's and I was hoping he could help me out with something."

"I'm not sure how helpful he's going to be seeing as how he's been dead for nearly a year. Maybe I can help?"

"Well great," Harmony said, walking further into the office and taking the small cluttered space in with a nod. "What about his partner . . . Henry, right? Is he still alive?"

Lexie waved at Henry's empty desk perpendicular to hers. "Still kicking, but he's out of the office right now. What can I help you with?"

"Do you handle the weird stuff?"

"Define weird."

"I saw a guy take his face off and put it on another guy's face and I think he then became that guy, leaving behind his faceless original body that he then burned to cover up the evidence. Does that count?"

"Yeah, that's pretty damn weird," Lexie motioned for her to take a seat. "Why don't you start from the beginning."

Harmony sat down, setting her bag on the floor next to her. "I work for a bail bondsman and I was running down a skip named Alex Morrison who had pretty much just fallen off the face of the earth about two months ago. He got arrested on a drug charge, but after that he missed all of his court dates and just vanished. We spent about a month or so looking for him with no luck. I got a call last week saying that someone saw him coming around his old place so I figured I'd check it out." Harmony reached into her bag, took out a laptop and set it on Lexie's desk.

"I'd set up a couple of remote cameras from the outside on the off chance I'd catch something and yeah, some weird shit went down." She opened a file and a low-quality video of a cluttered, empty bedroom filmed from outside came up. After a couple of seconds two men walked in, one tall, blonde, and chunky, the other shorter, more muscular, and Hispanic. They started talking, the Hispanic one looking all over the place and twitching away from everything in the room. The blonde walked up to a dresser right near the camera, opening drawers and methodically looking through them.

"What are they saying?" Lexie asked. The volume was high enough that she could hear that they were talking through the window but not able to make out any actual words.

"Not sure," Harmony said. "That's Morrison," she said, tapping the blonde one. "He'd been dealing so I'm assuming he lured the other guy in with the promise of bargain priced drugs. But here's where it gets weird."

In the video Alex waved the hispanic man over and then turned his back to him, still rifling through drawers. Facing the camera, he put one hand on his face and then twisted it. His face turned independently of his skull and then was pulled right off, leaving behind a smooth patch of skin with no eyes, mouth, hair or any identifying features.

"What the shit," Lexie murmured.

The other man, now only a few feet away, stopped as Alex got up, holding his neatly removed face in his hand. When he turned and the other man saw him he screamed loud enough to be heard through the window and tried to back away. Alex's free hand reached out, snagging him by the wrist and then shoved the detached face on top of his. The hispanic man's screams were muffled but still audible and his whole body stiffened. There was a second where the pale white face stood out but then it melted, fading down into the smaller man's features until it just looked like Alex was palming the other man's face. The awkward pose lasted only for a second before Alex's faceless body dropped to the ground, shaking the camera.

The Hispanic man looked down at the body on the floor and then seemed to apprise himself, the manic twitching and shaking replaced with the slow, calculated movements of someone trying on a new outfit. After a moment he turned and walked out of the room.

"You have got to be kidding me," Lexie said, looking up at Harmony. "What the fuck was that?"

"I know, right?" she said, smiling with an excited glint in her eye. "If that doesn't qualify as weir-d then I don't know what does. But wait, check this part out." She tapped the screen again. In it the Hispanic man returned, this time holding a small gas can. He poured some of the contents on the body on the ground and then began splashing it indiscriminately around the room as he backed out and into the hallway. After a couple of seconds light sprang up from below the camera's field of vision, followed quickly by black smoke. Harmony clicked the video off and closed the computer.

"Yeah, that qualifies alright. Then what happened?"

"I was parked down the block and when I saw he'd set the fire I got out and ran to see if I could get a glimpse at where the new guy, or the old guy now looking like the new guy, had gone but he was gone. I got back in my car and took off before the fire department came."

"Did you show this to anyone else?

"What am I, nuts?" Harmony said, putting the computer back in her bag. "I drove back to the office and pretended I was never there. After a couple of days I made a show of doing some more digging and lo and behold, Alex Morrison's house burned to the ground with him in it. Case closed."

"So what do you want us to do?"

Harmony raised an eyebrow. "What do you think? There's a guy out there pulling off faces and stealing identities. Literally. How are you gonna let a guy like that go? Let's track this guy down and put a stop to him. Isn't that what you guys do or have I been misinformed?"

"No. I mean, there's more to it than that," Lexie let out a flustered sigh. "It's just that Henry and I have a couple of things going on right now, but I'm sure we could fit it in."

Harmony raised an eyebrow. "We-ll I don't want to be a bitch but time is kind of of the essence. There's not a lot to go on and I want to get on this before this thing vanishes again."

"I get it," Lexie said. "Let me talk it over with him and I'll see what we can do."

"Here's my card," Harmony said, taking one out of her jacket and placing it on the desk. She also took a flash drive out of her jacket and handed it over to her. "I made a copy of the video for you guys if you want to check it out more. I've got some stuff I'm following up on tonight but give me a call once you've figured out what you want to do."

"Got it," Lexie said as Harmony got up and headed for the door. She hesitated for a second and then got up following her out past Martin's desk. When Harmony looked back Lexie gave a little wave, which Harmony returned with a nod and smile.

"Man, a guy that swaps faces? I've gotta see that," Martin said.

"Sure thing," Lexie said, turning to walk back into the office.

"Awesome!" Martin said, getting up to follow her only to have the office door slam shut in his face.

"That's not cool Lexie," Martin shouted from the other side. "Not cool at all!"

"Wait, we're going to what?" Henry said, hanging his overcoat on the rack by his desk.

"We're taking a case," Lexie said. She explained about Harmony's visit and then played the video that had been cued up on her computer. Henry watched it with deepening frown lines. When it was over he walked back to his desk without saying a word.

"Is there a problem?" she said.

"It could be," he said. "We don't know anything about this woman. For all we know she could be in cahoots with this face-swapper. Or the video could be faked."

"'Cahoots?' Are you a hundred? And the video isn't faked. I mean, it doesn't look faked"

"Neither did Jurassic Park," Henry shook his head. "I don't know, this seems like a bad idea."

"There's nothing wrong with this. We help her out and get rid of some sicko who's probably killed God knows how many people."

"But you don't know anything about her. For all you know, there could be dozens of these things and she could be one of them. We need to be sure"

Lexie clenched her fists under her desk. "Since when are we in the business of only doing things we're sure about, Mister 'Hey let's hypnotize our receptionist and see if a demon pops out.'"

"That's exactly why I don't think we should do this," Henry said, wagging a finger at her. "You want me to admit that I was careless? Fine. I let wanting to find out who we were dealing with override everything I've learned. Believe me, I understand wanting to put a stop to this thing, but we have to be careful."

"So that's it? We're just done with this?"

"I didn't say that, but I think it's a good idea for me to do some digging first."

Lexie stood up and put her palms on the desk, trying to keep her hands from trembling. Henry was aggravatingly calm. "She says that time is of the essence and I'm telling you that she seems legit. So what's the problem? You can't trust my judgment?"

"No, but I should meet with her myself. Just to be sure."

"So if someone brings something to me I've got to get permission from you before we do anything about it? That's bullshit. I thought I was your partner, not your fucking sidekick."

The calm in Henry's face gave way to confusion. "Is that what this is about? I didn't say that, I just think--"

"Forget it," Lexie said, yanking her jacket off her chair and scooping up her bag before heading for the door. "You sit around and do your fucking digging and I'll work with her myself." She stormed through the reception area past Martin.

Lexie wedged herself into a corner of the crowded train, tapping her foot so fast and hard it bordered on stomping. In the good old days, before monsters and demons and guys who tore their own faces off, she could just get in her cruiser and drive off as fast and free as she wanted. Those joyrides had been the only law-breaking indulgence she'd allowed herself, following every other rule and regulation to the letter.

It wasn't lost on her that if she'd bent a few more rules and told a few more half-truths she could be back home racing along the lakeshore to blow off steam, not crammed into a metal tube like a fucking sardine on the way to her tiny, overpriced apartment so she could pace around chock full of impotent rage.

She closed her eyes and took deep breaths until her stop and walked the rest of the way as quickly as she could without running. It was still warm, warmer than it should be for October, and as sweat began to trickle down the back of her neck and between her shoulder blades there was another twinge of irritation. Upstate it was probably cooler, and certainly no October humidity.

She stomped up the steps to her apartment, wrestled the lock open and then hurled her jacket against the wall. It flattened itself cartoonishly against the wall before dropping down onto the sofa. She darted over, picked it up and threw it back at the door. She sat down, dug her phone out of her purse and started dialing.

"This is Harmony," she said, picking up after a couple of rings.

"Hey, it's Lexie Winston."

"So what's the good word? There is a good word, isn't there?"

"Kind of," Lexie said, chuckling in spite of herself. "I can help you out with this but Henry is out."

"No kidding. Trouble in paradise?"

"Ugh, no. It's not like that. He's just . . . " Lexie trailed off, struggling for the words that fit him. Stubborn? Obstinate?

Cautious? The more she played their argument back in her head and heard her sudden and explosive anger the more a gnawing feeling of regret grew.

"He's just got a lot going on," she said, "So I'm going to be taking this one solo. Well, with you."

"Sweet, girl party" she said. "What's your schedule like?"

"I'm usually up at 6, so whenever's good for you."

"Ugh, mornings. Gross. I'm tracking down a lead right now but do you want to meet up later tonight? I think I'm on to something."

"Sure thing. Where?"

"I'll text you my address, but I'm in Queens so I can just pick you up at the train station."

"Okay. Sounds good."

"Sound more excited, Lexie," Harmony chuckled. "We're killin' monsters and bustin' bad guys. It's a reason to celebrate."

Lexie had been leaning on a signpost for ten minutes when a vintage red Mustang screeched to a halt in front of her and let out a quick bleat of its horn. The windows were tinted, and when Lexie walked around to the passenger side the door swung open for her.

"Your chariot awaits," Harmony said.

"Nice car," Lexie said, getting in and closing the door

behind her.

"It gets me where I need to go," she smiled. "And it goes really fast, which is a plus."

"I bet. So what's the plan?"

"We're supposed to have a plan?" Harmony said, shooting away from the curb and darting into traffic. Lexie felt her foot push down on an invisible brake and then eased off it with a sigh.

"You said you had a lead."

"I know, I'm just messing with you," she said, barely making it into an intersection before the light changed. "A cop buddy of mine ID'd the guy in the picture as Felix Marquez who'd been arrested a couple of times on some possession charges. I swung by his last known address which turned out to be his mom's house. His mom hasn't seen him since his run in with Morrison but his sister said a friend of hers ran into him at some club called the Panic Room in Astoria and he was acting really weird. I figured we'd check the place out and see if he shows again."

"Fantastic," Lexie grimaced, gripping the door handle so hard her hand went numb.

Harmony smirked at her. "Is my driving making you nervous?"

"That's one way to put it," Lexie said. Her phone started humming in her jacket pocket and she reached in to check to check it.

"Nice to see you came prepared," Harmony said, nodding at the Walther in the shoulder holster that came into view as Lexie took her phone out.

"We're on the job, aren't we?" Lexie said. It was Henry calling and her finger hovered over the "accept" button before she thumbed the thing to silent and tucked it back into her jacket.

"Was that Henry?"

"Yeah."

"Something wrong?"

Lexie sighed. "No, it's just...it's complicated."

"I can imagine. Is it monster complicated or personal complicated?"

"A little of both, unfortunately."

"Well that sucks. I can't imagine it being fun having a monster hunting business where you don't get along with your partner."

"It's not that we don't get along it's just that we're...different."

"Different can be good."

Lexie sighed. "Yeah, it can. And other times it can be a giant pain in the ass. So what's the plan once we find this thing?"

Harmony grinned and pointed at her in the universal "finger pistol" sign and mimed shooting her.

"So you're 'prepared' too?"

"Yup," Harmony said, patting her oversized purse that rested on the console between them. "I've been getting ready for this for a while."

"Your gun is in your purse?"

"What?" Harmony said, looking over at her. "No good?"

"It's fine if you think folks are going to wait for you to dig around in your purse before they try to kill you."

Harmony scowled at her. "I'm not a complete rookie, okay? I've been chasing fugitives for nearly five years now."

"That's great," Lexie said. "How many of them have you had to kill?"

Harmony turned her gaze back to the road.

"How many of them have you had to shoot?"

Still silence.

"That's what I thought. There's no shame in that, but this is a little different than running down bail jumpers."

"I get it," she said, the enthusiasm drained from her voice.

They took another corner, slower this time, and Harmony kept staring out at the road.

"Sorry," Lexie said after a couple of moments had passed. "I didn't mean to be a killjoy."

Harmony sighed. "No, I get what you're saying. Like I said before, my dad knew Henry's old partner and it wasn't just socially. My dad was in this life also, fighting monsters and all that jazz. I don't know when he started, but by the time I was ten he'd left home because it had become too dangerous for him to stay with us anymore."

"That sucks," Lexie said.

"Yup," Harmony said. "When my mom passed away six years ago he came back and explained everything to me, and that's when I realized I wanted to follow in his footsteps. But he took off again before he could show me. So I changed jobs, studied and got myself ready and I've been biding my time. And now," she said, tapping the steering wheel, "that day has come. Hence the reason why I'm a little over excited."

Lexie nodded. "I get it, but it's just a little weird finding someone who's super-psyched that monsters are real. I kind of fell ass-backwards into this life and Henry was there when I had nowhere else to go. I'm still not even a licensed PI yet so I can't go off on my own and private security doesn't exactly appeal to me. Not to mention the fact that once you know what's actually out there in the world the less likely you are to want to ignore it."

"Exactly," Harmony said. "Once you have monsters show up at your house in the middle of the night trying to kill your family you tend to over-prepare."

"In that case you should prepare yourself to carry your gun on you so you don't have to shoot anybody through your purse."

"Hey now," Harmony said, with a glare. "This shit's

Prada. No one's shooting through it."

"So are you going to call him back or what?" Harmony said.

"Hmmm?" Lexie looked up from her phone. Without even realizing it she been staring at it for several minutes, Henry's contact information up on the screen just waiting for her to touch "Call." They'd been parked down the block from the Panic Room for a couple of hours but it was still early enough in the evening that hardly anybody was showing up.

"I don't know," she said, stuffing the phone back into her jacket pocket, her face flushing with embarrassment.

"It's probably none of my business, but are you two...y'know?"

"No! Definitely not," Lexie snorted. "He's married. Plus he's not really my type."

"Oh, right right," Harmony said, nodding. "You're a little racist. I get it."

Lexie groaned and slapped Harmony on the arm, face flushing even brighter as soon as she realized that she'd done it. "Alright, alright," Harmony said, rubbing her arm with an exaggerated pout. "Take it easy on me, I'm little."

Lexie laughed it off and turned her attention back to the front of the bar with was conveniently facing away from Harmony. "But seriously," Harmony continued. "What's with you two?"

"There's been some weird stuff going on lately and…" she took a deep breath and then continued. "I think he's keeping things from me, like important business stuff. And I get that we've only known each other for about a year but it kind of sucks that he's pretty much the only person I know in the city. Well, no pretty much. He is. Him and Martin, but Martin doesn't count because he's kind of a weirdo. And I guess there is someone else but I'm beginning to think that was a bad idea."

"You know me. In fact, you're actually talking to me right now," Harmony said.

"Well I just met you."

"Sometimes those are the best people to talk to. But are you sure he's keeping important stuff from you and not just personal stuff? I mean, the two do overlap sometimes."

Lexie shook her head. "It could be, but if that's the case then he's going to have to decide if we're going to just be work associates or more than that. He's obviously been doing this a lot longer than I have and I can already tell that it takes a toll on you over time, but if you can't share that with someone that you're working with then who can you?"

Harmony nodded. "Yeah. For the longest time I never really got why my Dad took off. I knew that things were fucked up but I didn't really grasp why. Mom always told me not to be upset at him or blame him for leaving and it wasn't until he came back that I found out his reasons why. Maybe it's the same thing for Henry."

"I hope so," Lexie said. "I'm just going to call him and see what he wanted earlier." With a sigh Lexie hit call and waited for Henry to pick up.

"I was beginning to wonder about you," he said.

"I bet."

"So how's it going?"

"Fine. I'm out working on this thing with Harmony," she said, trying to match his tone with some difficulty.

"I figured as much. I've been doing a little bit of digging on this thing but I haven't had much luck so far. This could be somebody using some kind of artifact, a spell of some sort or just some creature I've never heard of. It's hard to say."

"I thought you weren't interested in this?" Lexie said.

"I never said that, I just wanted to explore all the avenues first. Unfortunately it's pretty slow going. It'd work better with two sets of eyes and I'd feel a lot better if you knew what you were up against."

"Well so would I. Get Martin to help you out. We're following up on a lead right now."

She realized that Harmony was staring at her with a raised eyebrow, fingers drumming on the steering wheel.

"Alright," he said with a sigh. "I'm still a little worried about all this, and--"

"We're fine. I'll let you know when we know more." She canceled the call and jammed the phone back in her pocket.

"'Not interested,' huh?" Harmony said. "I thought you said Henry was busy."

Lexie sighed. "Yeah, I know. He's just overly cautious, that's all."

"And from the sound of it he doesn't have any better of an idea on how to catch this guy than we do. Aside from reading up on him."

"Yeah. Are you still cool with this? It's your plan and your case."

Harmony shrugged. "It's our only shot. If he doesn't show tonight maybe we'll give something else a try."

Lexie nodded. "Cool. I'm sorry about Henry."

"Don't be. I was feeling bad that I didn't know enough to keep going with this but it's comforting that you guys are kind of clueless too."

As the flow of people into the Panic Room increased as the evening turned into night Lexie and Harmony realized that they were going to have to do their looking around on the inside if they wanted to make sure to have eyes on Felix. Once they stashed the majority of their weapons, they got in line and waited to be let in. They were worried that it would keep them from surveilling the rest of the folks waiting to get in but they were also worried that Felix had found a way to get in without them noticing. They both agreed that splitting up was a bad idea.

Inside the club was filled with stylish, upper-crust wanna-be twenty somethings that to Lexie just looked really awkward and bored with everything around them. The two parked themselves at a table with a sight-line to the door after making a quick circuit around the place to get the lay of the land. The music was so loud Lexie could feel it in her fillings and the near darkness punctuated by laser and strobe lights put her on edge. She couldn't tell what worried her more; that he'd already arrived and they missed him in the rush of people or that he wasn't going to show at all, making all this sound and light torture even more pointless than it already was.

"I'm pretty sure I've never seen someone look so unhappy," Harmony said, leaning in and yelling into Lexie's ear so she could be heard.

"This is not my idea of a good time. I've gone to more of these ridiculous places looking for monsters than I ever have on my own. Although I can understand why creatures from hell like places like this. It must remind them of home," Lexie said, turning slightly but still keeping her eye on the door.

"It's not that bad. I'd take a place like this over some redneck biker bar any day of the week, and I've been to plenty of those."

"Bikers aren't all bad," Lexie said, turning her head a bit more. Harmony didn't move and their cheeks were nearly touching. Lexie swallowed at the sudden dryness in her throat.

"They're mostly harmless and just trying to have a good time. There was a club back home that even did charity work with sick kids."

"That's adorable. Where's back home?"

"Selina. Upstate, by Lake Ontario."

She could feel Harmony chuckle but didn't dare to turn any closer. "I should've pegged you for a country girl. You should get up and stretch your legs. I talked to the guy watching the door, flirted a little and asked him to keep an eye out Felix."

Lexie cleared her throat. "Are you sure that's a good idea? Can we trust him?"

"Probably. I told him Felix was my ex boyfriend and that he was stalking me a little. If he thinks he can get all white knight on me then I'm pretty sure he's going to keep his eyes peeled. Besides, you sound like you could use a drink."

"I'd rather not. We need to stay sharp. Plus drinks in a place like this are ridiculously overpriced."

Harmony put a hand on her shoulder and maneuvered her away from the table. "Yeah, but if we get out, circulate and keep within sight of Greg the Bouncer we'll be okay. Plus we're cute girls in a club. Paying for drinks won't be something we have to worry about."

Lexie let Harmony lead her away, glancing back at the door and catching a glimpse of Greg the Bouncer, a six foot plus mountain of a man who nodded at her when they made eye contact. As the crowd grew thicker near the bar Harmony reached back and grabbed Lexie's hand, pulling her closer as she slid between pushy trendsetters. Lexie mumbled apologies but all she got in return were glares and eyerolls.

"Hey there," Harmony said when they made it to the bar, her voice loud and much higher pitched now. She pulled Lexie close, arm slipping around her waist. Lexie noticed that Harmony had undone another button on her shirt when she leaned forward to get the attention of a passing bartender. "Can my girlfriend and I get a couple of Heinekens please? We're really thirsty."

"Sure thing," the bartender said, grabbing a pair of glasses.

"Allow me," said a man in his late twenties, slipping in behind Harmony and flashing a white smile that stood out in contrast with the dark hair of his immaculately manicured beard. He reached into his suit jacket pocket and pulled out a pair of twenty dollars bills which he held out for the bartender, allowing his silver watch to "accidentally" peek out from the sleeve of his crisp white shirt and catch the light dancing around the club.

"Oh my god," Harmony said, taking the beers and passing one back to Lexie without even looking. "Thank you so much; you are such a sweetie!"

"I bet you are too. You and your girlfriend. I'm Evan. What's your name?"

"Not interested," Lexie said, leaning in and trying to put herself between the two of them.

"Hold on now," he smirked. "I paid your your drinks didn't I? I'm sure you could do something to pay me back."

"I can kick the shit out of you if you like," Lexie said, narrowing her eyes at him. "How about that?"

The wide-eyed innocent charmer look left Evan's expertly constructed face. "Fuck you, you fucking dykes." He turned and walked away, shaking his head.

"Jesus," Harmony said, her voice mercifully returned to its normal range. "You don't fuck around, do you?"

"Sorry," Lexie said, stepping back. "I just hate guys like that."

"Clearly," Harmony chuckled. "C'mon, let's get a better angle on the door and the crowd." She took Lexie's hand again and pulled her towards the dance floor. Lexie dug in her heels, nearly jerking the smaller woman backwards.

"Oh no," Lexie said, pulling her hand free. "Not a chance. I don't do...that."

"What are you, eighty? C'mon, it's just dancing. Get those long legs of yours moving."

"Not a chance," Lexie said, taking a step back. "You go investigate the dance floor, I'll cover the bar."

"Don't be such a pussy, c'mon. The last thing we want to do is lose sight of each other if we see him or Greg signals us."

"Ugh, fine." Lexie said, following her. They squeezed through crowds of people gyrating in various motions until they found a clear spot. Harmony started moving and swaying in ways that seemed incongruous with the wall of noise crushing in on them but watching Harmony made all the distractions around Lexie seem far away. After a second she realized that she'd have to start doing something so she shuffled her feet in a way that she hoped wasn't too ridiculous.

"Wow you really don't like this, do you?" Harmony said, sliding up against her and turning around slowly.

"I thought I made myself clear," Lexie said. "This is not a thing that I do. Ever."

"Oh my god, you're even biting your lip aren't you?"

Lexie opened her mouth, releasing her lip. "No. Maybe. Shut up."

"You are adorable," Harmony said, twirling around again and sliding her hands around Lexie's waist. "C'mon, it's not that bad is it?"

Lexie was unable to speak. She glanced up and saw Greg the Bouncer's giant paw raised towards her, waving. "Hey," she said, pulling Harmony's hands off her waist. "Greg's signaling us. Let's get to work."

"Ugh. So much for mixing business with pleasure."

The two pushed their way through the undulating crowd and found Greg waiting for them at the edge of the dance floor. "Did you see him?" Harmony asked, her voice going up into the annoying girl octave again.

"Yeah," Greg said, looking them both over. "He was trying to get in and I told him to go around the side for a VIP entrance and to wait there for me. I think he was dumb enough to believe it."

"Awesome," Harmony said with a wide grin. "Can we go with you? I really want to tell him off, and so does my friend here."

Greg nodded. "Sure thing. I got someone to cover my spot for me. If you want, I can call the police or--"

"Don't worry about it," Lexie said. "Just take us out there and we can handle this guy on our own."

Greg looked her up and down and then nodded again. "Sure thing, lady. Guys like that, they get what they deserve, y'know?"

"For sure, for sure," Harmony said, waving him on. "Let's do this thing."

Greg pushed through the crowd like he had a plow strapped to him and the two followed in his wake. They ducked through a door they wouldn't have even noticed near the bar and walked down a small access hallway filled with cases of liquor and glasses. Greg stopped at a door and waited for one of the bartenders to pass them before pushing the door open and gesturing around it.

"He should be right back there," he said, waving them past him.

"Awesome! Thank you so much Greg!" Harmony said, as Lexie stepped out into the alley. The alley was narrow, only about four feet wide and lit by only a bulb above the door. A few feet beyond the door there was someone slumped on the ground, a dark pool around its head and a bloody brick right next to it. Just as what she was seeing settled in her mind the door slammed behind them.

Lexie turned in time to see one of Greg's massive hands grab Harmony's head and smash it against the alley wall. She slid down to the ground, blood flowing from her temple and fumbling for her bag which had fallen behind her. Lexie lunged forward, jabbing at Greg's throat but he batted her arm away.

He swung one of his massive fists and she turned just in time, taking the blow on her shoulder and getting knocked back against the wall. Greg smirked, reaching out to grab her but she scrambled free and lashed out, punching him twice in the face. He shook them off and charged forward, driving Lexie back until she stumbled against Felix's body on the ground.

Greg's eyes lit up and he grabbed a handful of her shirt to steady her and then punched her in the face. The impact sent them both tumbling to the ground, him falling on top of her and nearly trapping her under him. She tried to scramble out from under him but he reached up to grab her throat first with one hand and then the other.

"I'd forgotten what it's like to be this strong," he said,

grimacing with effort as he squeezed. She reached up to gouge at his eyes but his arms were much longer than hers and he straightened up so that only the tips of her fingers brushed against his cheeks. He snapped at them with his teeth, almost playfully.

"I don't know what you're after and I don't really care," he snarled. "Then again, there's an easy way to find out." The snarl contorted into a smile and he took a hand off of her throat and placed it on his face. It shifted, tilting incongruously and then there was a metallic snap behind him. Greg's face slipped back into place and he turned just as Harmony swung her tactical baton into his cheek, knocking him backwards.

Greg cried out, his grip on Lexie's throat weakened, and the impact forced him back enough that she could get a leg up. She pushed herself out from under him and drove a booted foot right into his nose. He fell backwards, scrambling to get away from the two of them, blood flowing from his nose and eye already swelling shut. Harmony staggered towards Greg and swung the baton at him again. He lifted his forearm up and block it, grimacing in pain and then uppercutted her in the stomach so hard she lifted from the ground.

"Gahd dahhmit," Greg wheezed, trying to wipe the blood from his eye with the back of his hand while trying to shake off the baton's impact to the other. "Yhur fuggin dead."

Lexie reached down into her boot, pulled out a small tactical knife, and flipped open the spring loaded blade. "C'mon then," she said, her voice ragged. "Let me help you take that face off."

He wiped at the blood trickling down his face again, eyes going from the blade to Lexie and then back again. Harmony coughed and got to her feet, leaning against the wall for support. "Yeah, tough guy. Bring it," she said.

He stood for a moment and then turned on his heel and ran down the alley towards the front of the club. "Help!" he screamed. "Deez bitches are crazy! Dey killed dis guy!"

"Fuck," Lexie said. "We gotta go. Can you run?"

"We'll find out," Harmony said, shaking her head and trying to clear it. The two took off, running down the alley in the opposite direction.

"That did not go well," Harmony said, sitting on her kitchen floor and pressing a towel to her temple. The bleeding had almost stopped but the purple-black of the bruise had spread down to her eye.

"You think?" Lexie said, her voice mostly recovered but still a bit gravelly. The two had managed to circle around and get into Harmony's car before they heard any sirens and headed to Harmony's house in Queens, Lexie driving as Harmony gave groggy directions while trying to stem the flow of blood with her shirt.

"What are we going to do now?" Harmony said.

"I don't know," Lexie said, taking a sip of water and

leaning against the sink. Harmony's house was a narrow, single story ranch house that had been immaculately clean until the pair had stumbled in the door and dripped blood everywhere.

"Do you think they're looking for us? The cops, I mean."

Lexie sighed. "I doubt it. He was probably just trying to cause a distraction before he took off." She tried to believe it herself but she knew when the cops arrived there'd be a hell of a scene to investigate.

"He knew," she said, trying to pull herself to her feet. "Greg. The thing that looked like Greg. He knew that we'd talked, that we'd been looking for him."

"Yup," Lexie said, taking another drink and helping Harmony stand. She wobbled for a moment, leaning in to Lexie and then steadied herself against the counter.

"How did he know? Did he...ugh, shit I think I'm going to puke."

"He must be able to see the memories of the people whose bodies he steals."

"Jesus. That might have been nice to know."

"You think?" Lexie walked away, running a hand through her hair.

"Well, it could be worse."

"Just barely. The fact of the matter is that this guy is still out there and now he knows we're looking for him. He may not be done with us."

"Fantastic. So now what?"

Lexie sighed and took out her phone. "What are you doing?" Harmony said.

"Swallowing my pride," Lexie said, calling Henry. It rang several times before he picked up.

"Are you okay?" he said. He sounded tired but he answered so fast he probably hadn't been asleep.

"Yes and no," she said. She ran him through what happened, trying not to picture him rubbing his head with an exasperated look of disappointment on his face.

"That's not great," he finally said.

"Tell me about it. What's next?"

There was a long pause. "Do you think the police will be able to trace you?"

"Outside of DNA, I doubt it. Hold on," Lexie turned to Harmony. "Have you ever been arrested?"

"No," she said. Lexie nodded and went back to the call.

"They probably don't have her DNA on file so nothing will pop in the system if they test the spot where she got hit. Chances are they may think it's just Felix's blood. I think Felix crushed...I mean, what used to be Felix and is now Greg, crushed Felix's head to cover up the whole face removal thing."

"I wouldn't be surprised," Henry said. "I did some digging and I found a handful of murders that sound like they could be a part of this. From 1965 to 1971 there were five bodies found with faces neatly removed in a similar fashion.

Every one of them the cause of death was a severe shock to the system that stopped the heart."

"So that's what kills them."

"Exactly," Henry said. "I had Martin looking up other cases around the country after 1971, but he only found one in Memphis in 1982 before I sent him home. After that, nothing."

"So this thing has been around."

"Yeah. From what you said it's probably either a creature or someone using sort of artifact."

"Is that supposed to make me feel better?"

"It's a lead. Almost. What are you doing now?"

Lexie looked back at Harmony and then walked into the living room, lowering her voice. "We're just holed up at Harmony's right now. I doubt the cops will have a lead on us and I'm hoping that thing didn't follow us but I want to hang tight here to be sure. Other than that I'm kind of at a loss."

Henry was quiet again. "Do you want me to come out there?"

Lexie stopped and drummed her fingers on her leg. "I don't think so. Keep digging and maybe you'll find something."

"Ok. I'll poke around with a couple of the cops I know on the force and see what they think they found at the crime scene and make sure you two are clear."

"Okay, thanks," she said. "Henry...I'm sorry about yesterday."

He paused. "We'll talk about it later. I'll call or text you when I hear something. You two just stay safe."

"Will do. Bye," she said, ending the call.

"What's the good word?" Harmony said, leaning against the archway leading in to the kitchen.

"Pizza," Lexie said. "But since we don't have any of that Henry said he was going to check with some of his cop buddies to make sure we're not wanted for murder."

"That'd be good to know. So you're gonna crash here tonight? How forward of you."

Lexie felt her face flush and she looked away, trying to put her phone back in her pocket, missing at first and then finding the mark. "I just figured it was safer that way."

"I know, I'm just teasing. You're welcome to stay, especially since there's no one else I'd rather have watching my back. Get comfy, I'm going to change into something else."

"Okay," Lexie said, resuming pacing around the living room as Harmony walked back to her bedroom. The house was cozy, with plenty of pictures hanging on the wall of Harmony and her folks, a young Harmony at various dance recitals, and one in formal wear outside the house with a tuxedo wearing boy that had a look on his face like he'd won the lottery. The place was filled with a blend of old tchotchkes and furniture punctuated splashes of modern décor. Neatly fanned on the coffee table in the living room were an assortment of high fashion magazines.

"Getting the lay of the land?" Harmony said when she

returned, wearing short gym shorts and a small t-shirt.

"Something like that. So...how do you want to do this?" Lexie said, and Harmony raised an eyebrow.

"I mean," Lexie said, flushing again, "Do you want to sleep in shifts or out here or what?"

"I defer to the expert," Harmony said, dropping down on the couch. "I've done enough damage this outing. There's an office with a futon and a queen sized bed in the bedroom, plus this couch folds out. However you want to play it."

Lexie nodded. "Well, we should probably sleep in shifts just to be sure. Maybe out here, just so this thing doesn't sneak in and replace one of us."

Harmony nodded. "That's smart." She reached into her purse and took out her pistol. She'd expected someone of Harmony's small stature to have a similarly-sized pistol but it was a standard-sized Glock that managed to look extra large in her petite hands.

Lexie said. "No wonder you keep it in your purse. If you clipped it to your belt you'd topple over."

"Ha ha," she said, releasing the clip, checking it, and then slapping it back in place. "I figured if I needed to draw on someone I'd get something that could stop them in their tracks and nothing does that like .357 magnum."

Lexie sat down next to her, taking her Walther out of its holster and placing it on the table as well. "Do you shoot often?"

"Probably not as much as I should, but I'm okay."

"Well then you should know that if you're going to stop someone in their tracks you're going to have to hit them first. Accuracy trumps caliber."

"Well you're just a big know it all, aren't you? I bet I could learn bunches from you."

Lexie smiled a little. "Lesson one: Don't shoot at me. We'll work out the rest later."

"So you think this is going to be a regular thing?"

Lexie smile went away and she picked up her pistol to check it. "I don't know. Maybe, if this is something that you want to do more of and if Henry thinks we can use an extra hand."

"Oh, I get it. If Henry says it's okay. I see how it is."

"It's not like that," Lexie said, slumping back on the couch. "As aggravating as he is, if I'd have listened to him more then maybe things wouldn't have gotten this messed up."

"Yeah, because this is so terrible," Harmony said, leaning back next to her and elbowing Lexie in the ribs.

"There have been worse things," Lexie said, moving away from her.

"True. Besides, I probably was slowing you down."

"You did okay," Lexie said. "Cracking him upside the head like that kind of saved my ass."

Harmony grinned. "You were pretty bad ass with that knife of yours, being all 'Come get some' and making him turn tail. It was pretty cool."

"Alright," Lexie said, getting to her feet. "We should probably get squared away and rested. I'll take the first shift and you can rest up some. Plus I can wake you up just in case you've got a concussion or something."

Harmony watched her for a second and then shrugged. "Fair enough." She grabbed an afghan off the back of the couch and draped it over her legs as she stretched out on the couch. "I will warn you, I've been told I snore."

***

The car alarm went off at 4am.

Lexie had only been asleep for an hour and she sprung straight up off the couch, grabbing for her Walther. Harmony was already at the side window, looking out at the driveway.

"I can't see anything," she said.

"Shut off the alarm," Lexie said, heading for the front door. Harmony ran over to her purse, dug through it for her keychain and then thumbed the alarm off. Lexie watched the front of the house through one of the small windows in the front door and Harmony returned to the side window.

"We should go and check it out," Harmony said after a couple of minutes. "I can circle around the back and you can come up through the front."

"No," Lexie said. "As fast as that thing can replace us

96

there's no way we're splitting up."

"So what do we do?"

"We wait," She said. "Does your alarm ever just go off like this?"

"Nope."

"Then he's trying to draw us out. If he wants to get us he's going to have to come in here to do it."

Harmony snickered. "Well good luck with that. The house is alarmed too."

As if to confirm it the piercing shriek of the alarm went off and Harmony raced over to the keypad by the door. She punched in her code and it stopped. "Come on," Lexie said, tugging at her arm. She could feel it tremble and she stopped to look back at her. "Take a deep breath. And whatever you do don't shoot unless you are absolutely sure it's him, okay? And remember: don't shoot at me."

Harmony closed her eyes, swallowed hard and then nodded with a thin smile.

The two walked through the house, turning on the lights in each room, one checking the window while the other stood at the door watching. They were halfway through when the alarm went off again. They ran back to the front of the house, pausing as they entered the living room and putting eyes on every window and door before heading to the alarm panel to shut it off.

"This isn't good," Lexie said, standing at Harmony's

back.

"You think?"

The phone in the kitchen rang and the two walked over to it back to back. "It's the alarm company," Harmony said picking up the phone. "Tell them everything's fine," Lexie said.

Harmony nodded and answered. "Yeah, hi...no, we're fine...My cousin set the alarm off trying to surprise me...No, we're good...No, you don't have to dispatch anyone...Okay, thanks." She hung up.

"Now what?" Harmony asked.

"Turn off the alarm," Lexie said. "We don't need the distraction. Or cops. He's trying to rattle us."

"It worked. A+ bad guy menacing."

They walked back over to the alarm panel and Harmony keyed in the code to shut it down. The two stood silently in the living room, moving back to back again. There was a sound from the back of the house and Lexie could feel Harmony turn to head towards it, but she put a hand on her arm to stop her. They waited a few more seconds and the sound repeated itself.

"Follow me," Lexie whispered, leaning in close to Harmony's ear. "Watch our backs and remember, do not fire unless you know you have a shot." She felt Harmony nod and the two of them headed towards the back of the house, guns raised. Halfway down the hall they heard the noise again, a soft tapping from the office. Lexie nudged her and motioned with her head that was where the sound was coming from. Harmony nodded and the two moved to side of the open bedroom door.

Lexie motioned for her to stay back and she swung around, aiming into the room. It was empty, but as she exhaled evenly she saw that one of the blinds was swaying in the breeze and tapping on the window. Lexie frowned and raised her pistol. The windows had all been closed earlier.

The room was small enough to see everything and there wasn't much furniture, just a sofa along the other wall and a desk and chair under the window. Across the room from the sofa was a closet door, barely ajar and showing only a sliver of blackness. Lexie backed out of the room and nodded for Harmony to move closer. Lexie pointed towards the closet door with her gun and then tapped herself on the chest. Harmony nodded and Lexie motioned for her to keep an eye out.

The two crept into the room, Harmony backing up against the far wall and Lexie moving so she could open the door and be out of the line of fire. Harmony nodded that she was ready and Lexie yanked the door open and then backed away. The closet was jammed full of piles of boxes and old clothes. Harmony let out a sigh and walked over to the window before Lexie could signal her to stop. Harmony shut the window with a slam and Lexie caught a glimpse of something out of the corner of her eye.

She turned back to the hallway just enough so that the bat hit her across her back and shoulders and not her skull. The force of the blow slammed her against the wall and he swung again, this time trying to knock the Walther out of her hands, but she held on as hard as she could as the bat smashed into her fingers.

Harmony spun around, raising her pistol and Lexie could see the hesitation in her face as she tried to figure out if she could hit Greg and miss Lexie. Before she could figure it out Greg grabbed a handful of Lexie's hair and hurled her at Harmony. Lexie slammed into the smaller woman with such force that Lexie could feel the breath rush out of her in a massive gasp. Lexie tried to get to her feet but he swung again, this time catching Lexie's wrist with such force that the Walther flew from her grip. He grabbed her hair and flung her aside.

Greg swung at Harmony, hitting her across the stomach, doubling her over. She tried to bring her gun up but he kicked it from her grasp, sending it bouncing into the hallway. He kicked again at her head, spinning her around, leaving her motionless on her back with blood gushing from her re-opened wound. Lexie grabbed for anything solid from the desk and found a heavy coffee mug which she swung against Greg's skull with a scream of anger. It shattered in her hand and she could feel the bits of it digging into her palm.

He growled in anger and swung at her but Lexie ducked under the bat, punching at his midsection. He grunted in annoyance and swung with the bat again, landing a glancing blow on her shoulder that sent her reeling.

She sprung back at him, sending a flurry of punches at his face. He swatted her fists away but stumbled backwards. With a yell he dropped the bat and charged into her like a freight train, lifting her off the ground and the crushing her into the far wall. Everything in her body shook. Greg grabbed a handful of her shirt, held her against the wall and punched her in the stomach three times. She felt like she was going to vomit but there was no strength or air left in her body; the only thing holding her up was Greg's paw pressing her against the wall.

"This is no way to treat a guest," he said. Up close she could see that most of the damage they'd done to him had healed preternaturally fast, leaving behind only the faintest traces of bruising and a smattering of blood from where she hit him with the mug. "One of the perks I get from stealing bodies is a perfect recollection of their memories, Ms. Winston from Selina, New York. A pity you and Ms. Valley used your real IDs when getting into the club. Made it real easy to track you down once I healed up a little bit."

"Fuck you," Lexie gurgled, trying to squeeze out of his grip.

"Not interested," he said, pressing harder. "I'd like to think that you two cunts don't know anything about me and that you're just working on your own but I can't take that chance. This is New York, after all," he snarled. "I'd heard things were changing but I'm not going to take the chance.

There's only one way to be sure."

He reached up, grabbing his face and giving it a small twist. It turned and he lifted it off his skull, leaving behind a smooth and featureless flesh colored expanse. In his hand she could see Greg's face still intact, eyes twinkling with delight. When he turned it around she could see the back of it, red and wet looking, but underneath that it was pulsating and twisting. As it got closer she could see something reaching out for her, rows and rows of sharp, needle-like points twisting and spinning, desperate to burrow and feast.

She raised an arm, getting it into the crook of his elbow and keeping the thing from getting any closer. The featureless head tilted in annoyance and Greg's body shifted, pressing closer and forcing his forearm into her throat. She kicked at him but he pushed upwards on her throat, lifting her up on her toes. She jabbed at him with her free hand, trying to get him in the throat but it didn't budge him at all. The squirming, hungry mass on the back of the face was so close she could feel heat coming off it like it was a living thing.

Something moved behind him and she looked to see Harmony, grabbing for Lexie's Walther and turning to aim, blood running down her face and hands trembling. Lexie's eyes widened and she wanted to scream *Be sure!* at her but Harmony fired. Lexie winced, the bullet hitting the wall a couple of inches from her head and nothing else. Greg's body jumped at the gunshot and Lexie pushed the arm and hungry face further away, gasping for breath as his forearm left his throat. She tried to squirm free of the grip he had on her shirt but it was too tight. Greg's body turned to face Harmony, who had now scooted herself up against the couch, one eye squeezed shut so she could keep the blood out of it, and he pulled Lexie in front of it like a shield, arm moving up and grabbing at her throat.

"Face!" Lexie croaked, using both arms to push the arm holding the face above their heads.

Harmony nodded and fired, the first shot missing again but she second clipping the top of the face just above one of Greg's disembodied eyes. Lexie felt Greg's body shudder with pain and she kicked her heel up, knocking him backwards. The face dropped out of his hand and landed on the floor, looking up at Lexie contorted in rage and silently screaming at her. She stepped towards it, feeling Greg's fingers grabbing at her hair as she did. She lifted her leg high and stomped on the detached face with all the force she could muster. There was a muffled scream from behind her, and then Greg's body fell limply to the ground. Lexie kept stomping and she could see Greg's features fade away into a black, spongy mass. She could feel it pulsing under her foot, and she kept stomping until it stopped.

When it was done she felt her legs wobble and she managed to step away from it before her legs gave out, dropping her to the ground. She pushed herself over to the couch to lean against it next to Harmony. The two sat, catching their breath and staring at the black, broken mass on the carpet and the faceless corpse beyond it.

Lexie's throat was raw and every breath took more effort than it should've. After a couple moments she said "You shot at me."

"I shot near you," Harmony said, still not moving.

"Maybe you would've had better luck if you'd shot away from me."

"I saved your life, don't be a bitch about it."

"Sorry. I get bitchy when people shoot at me."

"Near you. And I missed."

"You missed a lot."

There was another long pause and then Harmony said, "What are we going to do about the dead guy?"

Lexie shook her head. "I don't know. But I'm working on it. Do you think your neighbors will call the cops?"

"Because of the gunshots?" she shrugged. "It's Queens. You never know."

***

"So let me get this straight," the cop said, peering down at Lexie. "This guy sets off the alarm a couple of times, you think it's her cousin but it turns out to be some random lunatic who then breaks in, attacks you both, you shoot at him and he gets away?"

"Do I have to repeat it? I'm a little hoarse," Lexie croaked. They'd managed to get Greg's body stashed in the crawlspace under the house before the cops arrived about a half hour after they'd made their own call to 911.

"You two always armed?" the cop said, motioning to Harmony who was getting examined by the EMTs they'd called.

Lexie nodded. "Most of the time. Old habit from when I was a cop upstate."

"No kidding," the officer said, not looking up at her but scribbling in his notebook. "Not a lot of PIs carry guns. Especially ones that aren't actually PI's yet."

Lexie bit back a response. "Like I said, old habit."

"And she did the shooting but with your gun, right?"

"Yup."

The cop kept writing. "Three shots, huh? And you didn't hit him?" he said, turning slightly to Harmony.

"They were warning shots," Harmony said. "I was trying to make sure I didn't hit her," she added, glaring pointedly at Lexie.

Nodding and writing, nodding and writing. "You got lucky," he said. "Small room, that many misses."

"She's very lucky," Lexie said, glaring right back at her.

"We've got to go," the EMT said. "She needs stitches and some x-rays."

"Fantastic," Harmony winced, getting to her feet.

"Alright," the cop said, closing his notebook. "I'll go ahead and file a report but like I said you girls got lucky. Guess he picked the wrong house, huh?"

"Yeah," Lexie said, taking Harmony's arm and helping her towards the door. "He fucked with the wrong chicks."

***

The next day, while Harmony was still in observation at the hospital for her cracked ribs and concussion, Lexie and Henry drove the Gremlin out to her place in Queens to retrieve Greg's body. She and Henry got it wrapped up in trashbags and into the trunk without anyone noticing. She'd kept the remains of whatever had been Greg's face (and probably countless other faces over the years) in a separate bag, and thankfully the cops hadn't lifted the small rug that covered the black ink stain the thing had left behind.

"Amazing," Henry said, poking at it with his pen.

"That's one word for it," Lexie said. "Now imagine it squirming right in front of your face trying to latch on. Less amazing."

"I bet," Henry said, dropping the remains back into the garbage bag. "I've never even heard of anything like this. Here's hoping it's just one of a kind thing."

"With our luck there's an army of these things out

there."

Henry shrugged. "I don't think our luck's that bad."

"That may be where you and I differ," she said.

Henry grunted. "Yes. That's where we differ."

Lexie had been heading out to the car but stopped. "What's that supposed to mean?"

Henry sighed. "Nothing. Do you want me to drop you off at the hospital?"

Lexie nodded. "Yeah, that'd be swell."

They rode there in silence for a while, Lexie tapping her hand on her knee impatiently as Henry drove until she couldn't take it anymore. "So what did you mean?"

"Bout what?" he said, not taking his eyes off the road.

"About how we differ. What's up?"

"What's up is that I'm tired. Long day yesterday. I had to go do the deposition for the Gaines' lawyers, reschedule the Martinson's interview, and then run all the back at the office to meet with a potential new client. Which I was late for."

Lexie bit her lip. "Well, it could've been worse. You could've had the shit kicked out of you and almost killed."

"And maybe that could've been avoided if you hadn't stormed off. Which, by the way, I still don't understand."

"What I didn't understand was that you seemed completely unwilling to help out with this thing that turned out to be a big deal."

Henry turned the car and then parked on a side street,

finally turning to look at her. "I just wanted to be cautious and not run off with someone we don't know anything about, especially since we're in the midst of a couple of other cases, including one where someone who tried to kill us knows all about us and we don't know anything about them. And if you'd waited and we'd done some digging into this whole thing then maybe you wouldn't have gotten nearly killed."

Lexie turned away. "Well, when you put it like that you kind of make me sound like an asshole."

Henry sighed. "You're not an asshole, I just...I just wished you trusted me a little more."

"Really? Trust you more? Are you kidding me? You keep secrets all the time! Every time I ask about a case from the past or where you getting some piece of information from or even where we're taking this dead body, you can't tell me. Or you won't."

"Part of this job involves keeping other people's secrets, Lexie."

"Really? How about how you hurt your knee? Because I know you lied to me about that. And whatever happened to you in that circle last month was more than just some spell going wrong. Not to mention you were never exactly clear about what made Owen go so fucking crazy. Or you you ended up in this line of work in the first place. Do I need to go on? Meeting you completely destroyed everything in my life and I agreed to help you because I wanted to do some good but also because I didn't have anywhere else to go and you act like I'm some kind of security risk!"

Henry started the car again. "I'm sorry. I'm sorry about all of that and how it's changed everything for you. I understand that and I went through some of the same things when my eyes were opened. But maybe you can accept the fact that some things are personal. That I'm not keeping secrets for secrets sake but because I'm trying to keep people safe."

"So just shut up and trust you, huh?"

"Just like I trust you. I figured we'd earned that from each other. I guess I was wrong."

***

When they got to the hospital, Lexie got out and Henry drove off without a word. In her room, Harmony was watching some reality TV show about brightly colored loud women but clicked it off as soon as Lexie came in. "Hey," she smiled.

"Hey yourself. So what's the word?"

"I should be out by tonight. I'll have to take it a little easy and miss some work, which doesn't make my boss very happy. I told him I was tracking down Alex Morrison and he was even less pleased that I didn't have anything to bring back to him."

"I could call Henry and we can drop Greg's body off

with him. That'll be something."

"So you got it out okay?"

"Yeah," Lexie said, trying to decide between taking a seat in the chair or on her bed. "Henry says he knows someone who will be able to take care of it but he was a little mum on the details."

"What a shock," Harmony grinned. "The man of mystery act continues."

Lexie shrugged. "I guess. The drive over here got a little...heated."

"Fuck 'im," Harmony said. "We were the ones that bagged a monster and nearly got killed doing it. I think we deserve a little slack."

Lexie nodded. "I guess. Well, I should head back. I just wanted to check up on you while I was in the neighborhood."

"Okay," Harmony said. "But when I get out of here and after I get my place straightened up you should take me out to dinner as thanks for saving your life."

Lexie flushed. "Only after you shot at me."

"In the course of saving your life. You were a veritable damsel in distress and I came to your rescue."

"I hardly qualify as a damsel."

"Well I'd like to see you again. Socially. Like, for dating," Harmony said, putting a hand on top of Lexie's.

"Are...are you sure? I didn't think that you, y'know..."

"Liked girls? Yes, I do. You, especially. Besides maybe

you can teach me how to shoot."

"If we're going to hang out together someone has to. It's the only thing that'll keep me safe," Lexie said, giving her hand a squeeze.

"I think we'll be okay. We make a good team."

Lexie nodded, and despite the unpleasantness that was most likely waiting for her there, by the time she got back to the office her face hurt from smiling.

Injuries of the Past

November

"So how have things been?"

Lexie shrugged, swirling the remains of her coffee. "Not too terrible. It was pretty tense for a couple of weeks but I think we've moved past it. Or at least we've learned to just not really talk about it and be able to work with each other."

Don Porter chuckled. "Well that's something I guess. Henry always was a little tricky. Could never quite figure him out."

"He's not all that bad," said Lexie. "I think I may have been a little hard on him."

"Really?" Don said, raising an eyebrow. "He didn't seem that fine in the video you sent me."

Lexie nodded again, turning her attention back to the coffee. Pastor Don Porter was an old friend of Henry and his late partner Owen McCabe. When Henry had attempted a spell to find a lead on someone supplying dangerous enchanted items to the untrained and unsuspecting the result had been disastrous. Henry found himself in a mental battle with whoever they'd been tracking while Lexie watched from the other side of a protection circle. She'd recorded the whole thing, and when she thought Henry was blowing her off about how serious the encounter was she sent the video to Don, the only other person in this unfamiliar city she knew with experience in these things.

Don's interest was enthusiastically piqued and he kept pestering Lexie for more information she didn't have. His calls eventually slowed but he tried again shortly after she and Henry had butted heads about how to handle their last case. She exuberantly vented to him, the primary theme Henry being a "hypocritical lying, sneaking, son of a bitch." In the wake of an anger hangover she realized what a mistake it had been and went back to ducking his calls. She thought she'd heard the last of him until he cornered her while she was walking to lunch.

"It's possible that video wasn't as bad as I made it out to be," she said.

Don nodded. "You didn't seem to think so at the time. You said it looked like he almost died."

Lexie shrugged. "But he didn't. And ever since then he's been fine."

"As far as you know."

"I spend almost every day with him in a small office, Don. Or in a small car. He may not be most open guy in the world, but I don't think there's anything wrong with him."

"And you say that with your years of dealing with the occult?"

She grimaced at him.

Don gave a thin, condescending smile. "I've been dealing with the forces of evil for almost exactly twenty years. I've been neck deep in it since the day Owen came to me when one of my parishioners found themselves being haunted by an inhuman spirit. My eyes were opened that day, like yours were only a year ago."

"And?"

"So you'll forgive me if I claim to have a little more experience about what I saw on that tape. Because if it's what I think it is there's more going on than just a spell."

"What do you mean?"

"Have you come across any instances of demonic possession?"

"No," she said.

He nodded. "I've seen my share. Don't let Hollywood fool you, the Catholics don't have sole dominion over exorcisms. They have their own specialized rites but there are others. Even non-Christian ones."

"Wait, do you think Henry is possessed? That's crazy."

"Possession can be a long, drawn out process, Lexie.

Some victims go for months or years being possessed without showing any outward signs. Often the demon will find a way to act without the victim even knowing it. It's possible that spell Henry tried may have forced the demon to show itself, which means there may not be much time before it starts to exert more influence."

"That seems like a bit of a stretch."

"Any more of a stretch than a man I've known for nearly twenty years flipping out so bad he gets himself killed?" He said, voice louder than Lexie was comfortable with.

"It wasn't really like that, Don," Lexie said, trying to keep her tone even. "I don't know what happened to him but Owen wasn't unhinged when I saw him. He was deliberate and methodical. He knew exactly what he was doing and one of those things was trying to kill me."

"And that's not the man I knew," Don said, slapping his palm down on the table, causing silverware and empty plates to jump with a clatter. People turned to look at them and Lexie leaned in so she could whisper sharply at him.

"Settle down! What happened to Owen doesn't have anything to do with Henry and this supposed possession."

Don took a deep breath, closing his eyes. When he opened them he spoke with the deliberate tone of someone trying to rein in their temper. "I knew Owen before he and Henry met. I have no doubt that he's a good man, but after he and Henry partnered up things changed a bit. Henry is much more comfortable using sorcery and other unholy methods and after they started working together Owen began to feel the same way. There was always something going on with Henry, something just under the surface that I didn't quite trust. He felt...wrong."

"Maybe you're just a little racist," Lexie said, taking a final drink of her coffee and pushing it away from her.

He half smiled, half snarled at her. "That's not it."

"Either way," she said, getting to her feet, "I'm done with this. I don't know what your beef with Henry is but clearly sending you that video was a mistake. I'm sorry you lost your friend but don't call me again about this. You and I are done." She reached into her wallet and threw some bills on the table. "Lunch is on me."

"I'm right about him," he called after her as she walked away. "I know you know it too, otherwise you wouldn't have come to me in the first place."

****

"Any plans for Thanksgiving?" Henry asked.

Lexie shrugged. "Not really. I think Harmony and I'll get together at some point but I'm not really sure what her plans are."

"It's weird being in a new relationship this close to the holidays," Martin said, leaning against the door frame leading out to his desk in the reception area.

"First of all it's not a relationship. We're just...dating. A little. And secondly shut up, no one asked you."

"I was just curious, that's all," Henry said, shaking his head. "I didn't want it to become a whole thing."

"No, it's fine," Lexie said. It'd been a little over a week since she'd met with Don and since then she'd redoubled her efforts to smooth things over with Henry, predominantly out of guilt for talking to Don behind Henry's back.

"What about you guys?" Lexie asked. "Any plans?"

Henry shrugged. "Just me and Monica and the kids. Her sister lives in Atlanta and can't make it up this year so it'll be nice and quiet."

Lexie nodded. "Good. Quiet is good. I'd thought about maybe heading back up to Selina but...well, I don't think my aunt is that interested in spending the holiday with me."

"Still nothing, huh?"

"I guess not being officially charged with murder isn't quite enough to clear things up with the fam."

"Whoa," Martin said. "When did you almost get charged with murder. I mean, I'm not surprised but still."

"Ha ha," she said, flipping him off. "It was back when Henry and I first met. They almost charged me for Owen's murder but it was eventually ruled a clean shoot. It did, however, get me fired and kind of make me look like a crazy person. So there's that that."

"Huh. Well, I guess it kind of worked out okay for everyone. Not Owen, I guess."

"Anyway," Henry said, clearing his throat. "Monica was wondering if you wanted to come over and have dinner with us, since neither one of us are going anywhere or doing anything special."

Lexie tapped her desk, looking down at it for a moment before looking back up at him. "I'll think about it. Like I said I'm not sure if Harmony has any plans but I'll check. Thanks though. And thank her too."

Henry nodded, giving a slight smile. "I will. We'd love to have you, and even Harmony too of she doesn't have anything special planned."

"Okay," Lexie said, giving him a genuine smile.

"Well," Martin said after a couple of moments. "I'll be unable to attend as I'll be reporting to the Green family compound in Cedar Ridge for the appropriate amount of guilt and recrimination about losing a respectable job and becoming an office assistant, especially in the light of my sister's recent promotion."

"He didn't ask you," Lexie said. "And isn't that just a fancy word for 'secretary'?"

"Ha ha," Martin said. "I just thought I'd avoid the awkwardness by explaining why I wouldn't be able to make it anyway."

"Yes, you absolutely avoided awkwardness. Good job."

"Y'know," he said, throwing his hands up in frustration. "You can be a real bi--"

"Ah ah ah," Lexie said, wagging a finger at him. "You don't want to finish that. Even if I am in a good mood."

Martin let out a sigh and walked back out to his desk. "Think it over," Henry said.

"I will," she said. "Thanks."

"Of course," he said. "We're partners."

She opened her mouth to say something. Maybe something about the argument, maybe something about Don, but she thought better of it and just nodded in appreciation.

****

"So she's not coming?" Monica asked.

Henry shook his head. "Harmony is having a Thanksgiving thing with some friends at her place so she's going out there."

Monica let out a sigh and carried the casserole out into the dining room. It'd been a week since his wife had told him to relay her offer and ever since then she'd asked every night if Lexie had an answer. Every night he told her that she hadn't confirmed or canceled yet, until yesterday when Lexie sheepishly explained her and Harmony's plans.

"It's fine," Henry said, following after her. "I said she was happy for the invitation but I'm fairly sure she'd rather

119

spend the time with the girl she's been seeing."

"The one you haven't met yet, right? The one who's father knew Owen?"

"Yes, dear. That one."

She turned, glaring at him. "Don't 'yes dear' me. I'm just trying to make sure that the two of you fix whatever your problem is."

"I know, I know," he said, putting his hands up in surrender. "And I told you, it's fixed."

"You think," Monica said, turning back to the table. "You thought everything was fine with Owen and look what happened. By the time you realized there was a problem it was too late. I don't want you to have to go through that with this girl."

He walked over to her, putting his arms around her from behind to halt her fussing over the table settings. "I know," he said. "And I'm not going to let anything like that happen again."

She turned around in his embrace to face him, the annoyance supplanted by genuine concern. "I hope so. It's important that we don't let things like this fester and turn into bigger problems. Lexie seems like a good person but this life and these things can wear on you."

Henry nodded. He'd met Monica after he'd found himself well-ensconced in the world of the supernatural but after he'd been through the worst of it and turned his life around. He'd been in the process of putting his life back together when he met her and started to work with Owen McCabe shortly after. When he decided he wanted to marry her he told her everything, from his darkest days to the real reason he and Owen had started working together.

"I know, but she's tough. She can take it."

"Just because she's tough it doesn't mean she doesn't need a friend every once and a while. And toughness isn't the be all end all of everything, you know. Sometimes you need to know when to ask for help," she said, staring pointedly at him as she slipped out of his embrace and continued to set the table.

"We're not just talking about Lexie anymore, are we?"

"You're the detective, you figure it out."

Henry's phone rang before he could retort and he stepped away to answer it. "Hey Don," he said. They hadn't spoken since Henry's birthday party and before that he'd last seen him at the small funeral service there'd been for Owen.

"Hey there Henry," Don said. "Happy Thanksgiving."

"And to you too. What's going on?"

"Nothing bad," he chuckled. "Just wanted to wish you a happy holiday and see if you and the family are up to anything special today."

"Not really, just the four of us this year. How about yourself?"

"Not much, just doing some work at the outreach center. Say, if you don't have anything special planned would it be alright if I swung by for a little bit? I had something I wanted to run by you."

Henry paused. "Sure. I thought you said there wasn't anything wrong."

Don laughed, harder than seemed necessary. "There isn't, just something I've been thinking about and wanted to talk to you about face to face, that's all."

"Okay," Henry said.

"Great. I'll talk to you later then," he said, abruptly hanging up.

"Alright then," Henry said, putting his phone back in his pocket. He walked back to the dining room area, where Monica was still setting out plates. "I guess we may have one more for dinner after all."

"Oh my God," his daughter Lilly said, bounding in from the hallway. "Is Johnny's fake girlfriend actually coming to Thanksgiving dinner?"

"Lillian," Monica said, pointing a stern finger. "What did I tell you about that mess?"

"Uggggh," Lilly said. "It's not my fault he's all hung up on some queer girl. It's just sad."

"Hey," Henry said. "That's not a nice thing to say."

"What, 'queer?' That's a totally okay word, Daddy. Pierre says that's what his Dads call it and the group at school is called the Queer Alliance."

John Churchill came around the corner from the

hallway and slapped the back of his sister's head. "No it's not, dummy. It's called the LGBT Alliance."

He darted out of the way as Lilly grabbed at him. "Daddy he hit me!"

"Enough!" Monica yelled, stopping her children in their tracks. "John, do not hit your sister! Lillian, stop baiting him! The two of you get in the kitchen and start rolling up silverware in the cloth napkins from the cabinet. Now!"

The two sulked towards the kitchen, muttering jabs at each other when they thought they were out of earshot.

"You don't think John actually has a thing for Lexie, do you?" Henry said, walking over to his wife.

"Oh honey," she said, putting a hand on his arm. "I think he's more than a little smitten. You saw how he kept asking about if she was coming for dinner or not."

"Huh," he said, rubbing the thin fuzz of hair on his head. "I guess I didn't put it together."

"That's my detective," she chuckled. "He's smart enough to not do anything foolish but I don't think he can help having a little crush."

"Should I talk to him about it?" he asked, trying to keep from wincing.

Monica laughed. "Despite everything I said earlier, I don't think this is the kind of thing that needs to be talked out. It's a crush, he'll get over it. I think you're safe. "

****

It was a little over an hour later, the turkey almost done, when Martin called. He was nearly frantic with excitement and it took all of Henry's patience to calm him down and get him to explain it slowly. As he did Henry wandered towards the back of the apartment away from the rest of his family.

"So this is it," Martin said, breathless from the rush of information. "It is, right? I didn't get all worked up for nothing did I?"

"No, I think this is it. Good job Martin. You didn't have to stay on a holiday to do it though."

"No worries, man. The less time I spend with my family the better. And if I tell them I was staying late and working hard they may not give me grief. Or slightly less grief. Either way, this is preferable."

"Okay. We'll talk about this more on Monday and plan our next move from there."

"Can do, boss." Martin paused. "You haven't told Lexie about this have you?"

Henry sighed. "No, I haven't. And that was a mistake. I didn't want to get her hopes up especially since my last idea turned out to be such a disaster."

"Do you want me call and tell her? I was gonna do the Happy Thanksgiving text thing at least?"

Before Henry could answer the apartment buzzer went off. "No, I can do it."

"Did she change her mind and come over?"

"No, that's an old friend of mine. He wanted to stop in and ask me about something."

"Cool, so I--"

"Daddy! Don is here!" Lilly screamed down the hallway at him.

"Thank you, but you don't need to shout."

Martin chuckled. "Okay man. I'll let you go. Happy Thanksgiving."

"You too, Martin. Have a good one." Henry closed the phone and headed back out to the living room. John and Lilly were watching TV and Monica poked her head out of the kitchen. "I don't think we're going to be ready to eat for another half hour or so. Is he staying that long?"

Henry shrugged. "I'm not sure."

She grumbled in irritation and went back to work. Henry went to the door and opened it right as Don knocked.

"Happy Thanksgiving," he said with a smile, brandishing a plate of brownies as he walked in.

"To you to, Don," Henry said. "How're things?"

"Good, good," he said looking around. His gaze hovered on John and Lilly on the couch before scanning the rest of the apartment. "Is Monica here?"

"Right here," she said, coming out of the kitchen. "You

caught us a little early. Pretty much everything is done except the turkey."

"I thought that might be the case," he said with a relieved grin. "So I brought these." He held out the plate of brownies, smile growing wider. "I made them myself. Thought it might be nice to have something sweet to snack on in the meantime."

"How thoughtful," she said. "Lilly, can you get some plates for us please."

"Yes ma'am," she said, getting up and heading into the kitchen.

"Fantastic," Don said, handing Monica the plate and taking off his coat. John stood up to take it but Don waved him off. "No need, I can do it."

"Sure thing," Henry said. "Right this way." He led him around the corner to the hall closet, which he held open for him as Don hung up his coat.

"So what's going on," Henry asked, lowering his voice.

"Nothing major, don't worry," Don said, patting him on the arm, grin still wide. He walked back out to the living room where the kids were devouring brownies.

"These are delicious," Monica said.

"An old family recipe. I don't get to bake often but I figured this would be a perfect opportunity."

Henry picked one out for himself and took a bite, nodding in approval. "She doesn't usually like me having sweets like these," he said, indicating towards Monica.

"It's not my fault that diabetes runs in your family."

"Delicious, delicious diabetes," Henry chuckled.

"Well I'm glad they're appreciated," Don said. "So how are things Monica? How's the practice?"

"Well, you know what they say. It makes perfect," she chuckled.

"How about you guys? School going well?"

Lilly shrugged. "Alright I guess. I'm taking Pre-Calc this year and its lame."

"I bet," Don nodded. "I never was particularly good at that kind of thing. How about you, John? Must be getting close to time to think about colleges."

John nodded. "Yup. I'm thinking about NYU but my grades may not be good enough."

"Any idea what you want to do?"

John shrugged. "I'm leaning towards pre-law, but I'm not entirely sure."

"Thinking of following in your mom's footsteps, huh?"

"Maybe. I dunno."

Don nodded. "Well, you never know. Of course, you could follow in your Dad's footsteps. Wouldn't that be something?" Don laughed.

John shrugged, looking briefly over at Henry. "I dunno. I never really gave it much thought."

"Well," Don smiled. "Fighting demons and the forces

of evil is a pretty noble profession if you ask me." Henry stopped chewing and Monica glared at him. John laughed uncomfortably, looking over at his parents in confusion.

"I think he's just joking around," Henry said. He took Don by the arm and pulled him off to the side. "Don," Henry said, lowering his voice, "why don't we talk back here?"

"But this is important," Don said, keeping his voice raised and pulling free of Henry's grip. "You're doing noble work, it's nothing to be ashamed of. Unless you feel like you've got something to hide."

"What's...what's he talking about, Dad?" John said. His eyes were heavy-lidded and it looked like he was fighting to keep his head up.

"It's a joke," Monica said, glaring at Don. "I think it's time..." she took a step and then wobbled on her feet. She put a hand out for one of the chairs near her and grabbed it to keep from falling over.

"It's alright," Don said, taking hold of her shoulders and then easing her down into the chair. "Everything is going to be fine."

Henry took a step forward and felt his body wobble underneath him like jello. "What did you do?" Henry said. He looked over at John and Lilly on the couch. Lilly's head was lolled to the side and her eyes were nearly closed. Next to her John was struggling to stand up but seemed unable to get his balance.

Henry concentrated hard, focusing himself on taking first one then two steps forward. John watched, his struggling having stopped and now just staring over at his father and taking slow, deep breaths.

Don stared at Henry in grim amusement, a hand resting on Monica's shoulder. She was looking up at Don with slack jawed horror. "Don't...," she said, the word stumbling out of her mouth.

"It's okay," Don said, patting her shoulder and keeping an eye on Henry, who was still struggling to make his way over to him. "I'm not going to hurt you. Or the kids."

Out of Don's line of sight, John fumbled for his phone, which was sitting on the armrest of the couch next to him. He managed to knock it into his lap and began tapping at it with hands that looked like they'd lost all sense of feeling.

Don turned, trying to follow Henry's line of sight but Henry called to him, drawing his attention back. "If you hurt them," Henry said, each word coming out painfully slowly, "I will kill you."

Don turned his attention back to Henry with a small smile. "I have absolutely no doubt that you're capable of that," Don said, walking over to Henry. "That's the whole reason this is happening." Don reached out and gave Henry a shove backwards sending him crashing to the ground and into unconsciousness.

Lexie hated being late. Then again she also hated meeting new people in weird social occasions and the nebulous social niceties and expectations that came with it. Those kind of things led to obnoxious questions like "What should I wear?" and "Should I bring something?" and "I like guns. Can I talk about guns?"

After several false starts with a wardrobe that seemed painfully limited she settled on a pair of plain black slacks, a designer t-shirt and a light blazer. "It's not formal, don't worry about it," Harmony had said when she saw the reluctance on Lexie's face when she invited her to her "friendsgiving."

"Jordan's parents moved to San Diego, Cindy's folks are dead and Kevin's folks were fine with him coming out until he got a boyfriend. So we just get together at Cindy and Ron's in Pleasantville every year. It's one of the only times we get to see each other and I thought it'd be nice for you to meet them and not spend Thanksgiving alone."

"Henry did invite me to his place."

"Wow, he's actually willing to have you over? Did you pass the background check?"

"Very funny," Lexie said. Even with assurances of casualness, she found herself faced with near crippling indecision about things she'd hardly ever given a second thought, which lead to her current battle with punctuality.

After deciding on the train into Manhattan that she should bring something and that something should be alcoholic (for her benefit as well as theirs) she found herself standing in a liquor store staring at an overwhelming range of options.

"Wine," she muttered to herself. "City people like wine."

She took out her phone to text Harmony and see what kind they'd want when she noticed a missed call and voicemail she hadn't had when she left the apartment. It was from John Churchill, which was surprising given that aside from playing games they'd texted a couple of times but never actually spoken on the phone.

She wandered away from the wall of confusing wine and listened to the message. It was quiet at first and then there was sound like someone talking far away. Then there was a second voice, louder but sounded like the croak of someone with laryngitis trying to talk. There was a rumbling, like someone running, followed by the clatter of someone dropping the phone and the call ended.

She stared at her phone and walked over to one of the empty corners of the store. She placed a hand over her free ear and listened to the message again. The first word almost sounded like her name but the second was easier to make out now.

It was "Help."

She couldn't tell if it was actually John or not. The message was left about 45 minutes ago, which was right around when she was in the train under the river. She called him back but the phone just rang until it went to voice mail. She hung up before the greeting was done and contemplated her phone once more.

She called Henry's phone. It rang and also went to voicemail. She stared at her phone as she drifted towards the door of the liquor store and when she got outside she called Martin, tapping her foot impatiently.

"Happy Thanksgiving, boss lady. What's up?"

"Have you heard from Henry today?"

"I called a little while ago, why?"

"I got a weird message from his kid and neither he or Henry are picking up. What was going on when you called?"

"I dunno, they're probably having dinner or something and turned their phones off, it's--"

"Martin! Just listen to me, okay? I think he said 'help,' but quietly, like he was trying not to be heard. Just tell me what was going on when you called, okay?"

"Okay, sure. Um, he told me that you weren't coming over and...oh man, he said someone else was coming over instead. Some old friend."

"Who?"

"Ummmm...it was a guy. Short name. He didn't say but I heard Lilly yell it in the background. Not John...Ron maybe?"

Lexie swallowed hard, her body suddenly rushing with panic-induced adrenaline. "When was this?"

"Like an hour ago. Maybe a little more. I can check if you--"

"Nevermind," Lexie said, pushing her way out of the crowded store and walking briskly down the block, looking for a cab. "This could be really bad, Martin."

"Fuck. What can I do?"

"I don't know," she said, catching sight of a cab down the block and across the street. She broke into a run, hopping up over the corner of a car to keep from getting hit. "I'm going to give Harmony your number and if she calls you get over here and let her into the office and show her all of the potent shit. Okay?"

"Yeah, sure but...shit Lex I'm on a train in Jersey, it might take some time to turn around."

"I know. Give me an hour, okay? Then head back."

"Of course. Good luck."

"Hopefully I won't need it," she said, ending the call and skidding to a stop in front of the cab to stop it. The cabbie layed on his horn but she put up her hands apologetically before darting over and sliding into the back.

"Sorry man, but I need to get to 118th and Riverside drive. There's an extra $20 in it for you if we get there in 15 minutes, okay."

The cabbie looked back at her apathetically through the rear view. "Okay miss but is lots of traffic. May be longer."

"Fast as you can."

"Okay lady," he said.

Lexie took out her phone and called Harmony, taking deep breaths to calm herself down as the phone rang. "Let me guess, you're running late. Are you lost?"

"No it's...look, I've got to swing by Henry's real quick."

"Are you serious? Babe, they're gonna be serving soon and everyone wants to meet you."

Lexie sighed. "I know but...look, I think something's wrong with him. I need to check it out."

"Wrong? How could you tell?"

"This is serious, okay? I'm really sorry, but if this is what I think it is, it's my fault. I'm going to text you Martin's number and if you don't hear from me in an hour I want you to call him and he'll let you into the office."

"Jesus," Harmony said, lowering her voice. Lexie could hear her walking away from the noise of people in the background. "How serious is this?"

"I don't know. That guy I told you about, Don? I think he went to Henry's. I don't know what he might do but the way he was talking the last time I saw him he's not going to go over for a friendly chat."

"Lex honey, how serious could this guy be? Maybe he's just going to yell at him and ruin their meal. That's not an emergency."

"I know, I know, but I have to check. This guy has dealt with...things before. He may have something up his sleeve, and he's definitely convinced Henry is responsible for Owen's death."

"But he's not, is he?"

Lexie paused. "No, he's not. But I don't think that that'll matter to Don."

"Alright, you're freaking me out. I'm just going to come down there."

"No, don't. It could be nothing. Just wait for my call, okay?"

Harmony sighed heavily. "But if I don't hear from you break into the arsenal of occult weaponry and go in guns blazing. So no worries, relax and have a good time."

"Exactly. Talk to you soon."

"You better. Good luck, babe."

"Thanks," she said, hanging up. The cab was zipping uptown at an impressive speed despite the holiday traffic, but Lexie had a feeling that it wasn't going to be fast enough.

"Henry? Henry, I need you to wake up." The voice was calling to him through a warm, gauzy haze that was cradling his head. Something tapped his face and he flinched away.

"Come on, Henry. We need to talk." The thing tapped his face and he tried to slap it away but he couldn't move his hands. His eyes fluttered open, trying to figure out what the problem was and he realized he wasn't laying in his bed like he'd thought but sitting in a chair with his hands tight against the arms.

"There we go. Are you awake now?" Henry shook his head, trying to focus on the face in front of his. He tried to say something but his body seemed light years away from his brain.

"Need help? Okay, here we go." There was a snap of something close to his face and the air in his nose suddenly burned. Everything fell into focus, from the pain in his wrists from being tied together to Don's face peering at his at an uncomfortably close distance.

Henry lunged forward but he was held firmly in place. "Easy there," Don said, straightening up and letting out a nervous chuckle. "I know it's hard but try to calm down. Struggling is only going to make this harder."

Henry looked around. He was in the center of his living room, sitting in the high-backed chair from his bedroom. His wrists were tied to the arms of the chair with zip ties, his ankles were bound to the legs, and there was a belt cinched tight around the middle of his torso holding him to the back of the chair. As he struggled against the exceptionally tight bonds he heard the crinkling of plastic underneath him. He craned his neck to the side and saw the chair was sitting in the middle of a large clear tarp.

"Where are they? If you hurt my family I swear to God I will kill you."

Don chuckled. "Funny you should say that. But I'm not a monster, Henry. Your children and your wife are safe, still sleeping off the effects of the drugs. You have my word that they won't be harmed. This is between us."

"What is? What the fuck do you want?"

"I just want to help you."

"This," Henry said, waving his hands as much as he could, "is not helping me."

Don nodded, smile fading away. He got up and walked out of Henry's range of vision, plastic crinkling underneath him. Henry could hear him fiddling with something and then the noise stopped. There was nothing for several moments and then he heard him coming back.

He was carrying a small attache case in one hand and the plate of brownies in the other. He sat down on the couch, placed the brownies on the arm and took a small bundle of musty looking cloth out. He set it next to him and then took a brownie from the plate. He took a bite, closing his eyes to obviously savor the taste.

"Don't worry," Don said after swallowing. "I made a small batch of ones that didn't have any drugs in them. They really are a family recipe and I just couldn't imagine Thanksgiving without them. Which reminds me, I turned the oven off since the turkey looked just about done. I'm sorry to disrupt your dinner, but we all know the best part is the leftovers." Don looked at Henry with regret for the first time since he'd arrived. "I hate the idea of ruining the holiday but it took me a while to get what I needed and once I did I didn't want to wait too much longer. Time is of the essence. Besides, there was a better chance we wouldn't be interrupted by your partner. And who knows, maybe we close out the night watching football and eating turkey sandwiches."

"I doubt it," Henry said, trying to keep the strain out of his voice. The ties may be tied tight but the chair was an antique from Monica's family. He knew the wood was weak and the joints were barely holding together. If he couldn't break the plastic he could possibly pull the chair apart.

Don nodded in agreement. If he noticed Henry's hand gripping the arm of the chair and straining in effort he didn't show it. "You're probably right. Either way, today won't be a total loss."

"Just tell me what you're trying to do."

Don looked at him with incredulity. "I'm trying to save your soul, Henry. And make sure no one else dies because of what's inside you."

Henry stopped pulling on the arm of the chair and gave Don his full attention. "What are you talking about?"

Don leaned forward, all traces of humor gone from his face. "You're possessed, Henry. There's a demon inside you and I think it's been there for a long time. I think it's why Owen was killed."

Henry stared at him, taking in the utter conviction all over his face. "Don, you don't know what you're talking about."

"Don't I? How many times have you called on me to

help you because of what I can do? I can channel the power of the Lord into something you can use to fight evil. That's not something any theologian or clergyman can do. There's a reason behind it and Owen saw that. That same gift has given me insight, and the more I reflect and pray on it the more I see that there's always been something about you that's made me uneasy. Something just not right."

"Maybe you're just racist."

Don chuckled. "That's what she said, but I think you've done something to her. Changed her mind somehow."

"Who? Lexie?"

Don nodded. "She saw something, and she showed me. That's what started me on this path and confirmed what I think I always knew. That there's evil inside you."

"What the hell are you talking about? What did she show you?"

"She showed me the video of that ritual you performed a couple of months ago and what happened to you during it. I knew you dabbled in the black arts but that wasn't just some spell. What happened was demonic, pure and simple."

Henry raised and eyebrow. "Black arts? Like rap music and soul food?"

"Shut up!" Don yelled, getting off the couch and beginning to pace around the room. "You're just trying to confuse me."

"I don't have to try," Henry said. "I think you're

confused already. I'm not possessed, Don. I've touched the things you've blessed, I've been in the room when you've banished demons and none of that has affected me. How could I be possessed if all those things are true?"

Don turned back to face him and for the first time Henry could see the flickers of doubt in him. "I don't know. Maybe it's something else, maybe something more than possession. Maybe one of your spells or something more deliberate. Either way, I'm going to fix it. I'm going to save you. I'm not going to lose anyone else."

He walked back over to the couch and unrolled the bundle of cloth he'd taken out before. There was a metallic jingle as he lifted it up and then set it on the floor next to Henry. Looking down, he saw that the cloth roll had a series of pouches in it, and in each one there were various old, silver instruments of varying sizes and shapes. Some were blades, some were hooks, some were needles. All of them seemed to be engraved with tiny runes and all looked very sharp.

"Don," Henry said, trying to keep his voice even. "What are you going to do with those?"

"They were a gift from Owen," Don said, getting up and walking out of Henry's field of vision. As soon as he was out of sight Henry put everything he had into pulling at the arms of the chair. The right wobbled and the left listed a little but didn't budge any further.

"He gave them to me shortly after he introduced me to

you. I've only used them once on a case he and I took shortly after Lilly was born. A nasty affair with a witch upstate that was pretty unpleasant. I don't know where he got them, but he told me they were crafted during the Inquisition and created for extracting information from the vilest of infernal creatures. It may be a little overkill for our purposes but we'll have to make do."

Henry put all of his force into pulling at the arm on the left, pushing it as far as it would go and straining with effort. He heard Don dragging something across the floor and on to the plastic but didn't stop, feeling the arm beginning to bend a little more.

"Don't make this harder than necessary," Don said, suddenly at Henry's left, clamping a hand over his. Don's grip was stronger than Henry expected, and in a fit of desperation he twisted his hard around as much as the restraints would let him, took a hold of Don's hand, closed his eyes and whispered the words of a spell.

He wasn't sure if it would work, given how fuzzy his head still was from the drugs and how much he'd just been exerting himself but it was the only play he had left.

He felt the magic rush through him and he already knew it wasn't going to be enough. Don staggered, dropping down on one knee, eyes fluttering for moment as he shook his head, trying to fight off the wave of exhaustion that the spell caused.

"Wha...what?" Don stammered, yanking his hand from Henry's and trying to get his bearings.

"A spell," Henry said, trying to push against the loosened arm of the chair but the energy spent from the spell made him twice as worn out as he was before.

"I knew it!" Don said, backhanding Henry across the face. He pulled himself to his feet as Henry dabbled the corner of his mouth with his tongue, tasting blood.

"You hit a lot harder than I thought, Don."

"And I never would've thought you'd try to put some kind of demon curse on me. I guess that makes us even."

Don walked behind Henry, taking the dining room chair he'd gotten and placed it directly in front of Henry. He sat down and picked the bundle of torture implements up off of the floor and set them on his lap.

"You don't have to do this, Don," Henry said, putting what strength he had left into trying to snap the now seemingly immobile left arm of the chair.

"I'm not just doing this because of what happened to Owen but to save your wife and your children. Even Lexie."

"I had nothing to do with what happened to Owen!" Henry screamed. "I don't know what changed him! I wish I did and that I could've saved him but I couldn't!"

"And now he's dead." Don took one of the long slender knives out of the bundle and examined it closely.

"It wasn't me," Henry said, trying to brace himself for

what was going to happen next. "It doesn't matter who it was, does it? All I can say is that I'm sorry that I let our friend down."

Don set the blade down on his lap and looked Henry in the eye. "Henry, if you can tell me honestly that you have never been in league with demonic forces, that you've never used them for your own means and that your soul is unmarked by them then I will let you go right now and turn myself into the police. Can you do that?"

Henry stared at him, holding his gaze. "Do what you need to do, Don."

He picked up the blade. "Lord give me strength."

"Come on, man. You're killing me." Lexie said, tapping on the glass separating her from the driver.

The cabbie glared back at her in the rear view and waved at the stopped traffic in front of them. "Is holiday. Nothing I can do miss."

"Yeah, yeah," she said, sitting back in her seat and peering out the window to see what street they were on. It was 101st and it'd taken them nearly a half hour to get this far. At this rate it'd be another 15 or 20 minutes to go the rest of the twenty blocks.

She leaned up and tapped the window again. "I'm getting out here, okay?"

"Fine, fine. Please do not tap on glass." She shoved

some bills at him and as soon as he counted to make sure it was enough she hopped out. She walked half a block before she started going faster. By the next block she was jogging.

When she was at 103rd she started running.

Henry refused to scream. He bit his lip, grunting in exertion against the pain of the shallow cuts Don was making along his arms and the tops of his thighs. He almost broke when the first of the needles went in, Don turning and twisting it as it sunk nearly three inches into his thigh, right up to the silver hilt with intricate engravings.

With every cut and every needle Don murmured prayers to himself, focusing entirely on the work at hand. No matter what he wouldn't look into his face. Henry could hear drips of his blood landing on the plastic tarp like light spring rain. He'd lost track of how much time had gone by but there were at least two dozen cuts of varying lengths all over his body. His shirt and pants lay in tatters and the only blessing that Henry could see thus far was that Don hadn't started on his face yet.

Or opened his shirt any further.

After sinking a needle deep into the meat of Henry's shoulder Don finally met his gaze when he finished his small prayer. "You can feel it, can't you? I knew I wasn't wrong. There is something in there and this is hurting it, isn't it?"

"All you're hurting is me," Henry said, gritting his

teeth. "Stop this. Please."

"This is working, Henry I can feel it. I know you can feel it too."

Henry shook his head even though Don wasn't wrong. With every cut, with every needle, there was an extra bit of pain twisting around inside of him. Wherever Owen had gotten these implements, they were authentic and the damage they were doing was far more than just the cuts in his flesh. What made it all the more painful was the fact that no matter how effective they were, no matter how much Don cut and stabbed, they weren't going to do what he hoped.

"You're lying," Don said, wiping the back of his hand against his cheek and smearing a little of Henry's blood on it. "I don't know why you're holding on to it but you need to just let it go, Henry. Whatever this thing has promised you, whatever powers it's granted you, they come from a place of evil. It doesn't matter what good you've accomplished with them and what good you think you'll be able to accomplish in the future. Your very soul and the souls of everyone around you is in jeopardy. Please. Just let this end."

"You don't know what you're talking about," Henry said.

Don let out a heavy sigh. "Very well, let's keep going then." He reached out and started unbuttoning Henry's shirt.

"Wait! Wait!" Henry said, thrashing with what little effort he could muster and as much as the bonds on his wrists, ankles and around his waist would let him. Don stopped, fingers still at his the third button on Henry's shirt. He narrowed his eyes and unbuttoned it, revealing the tattoo above Henry's heart.

"Well, well," Don said, examining the circle with the intricate symbols all around it. Don reached back for one of the smaller, more delicate blades and touched the edge of the circle with its tip. He jerked back like he'd been shocked and Henry could feel the feedback all the way through his bones. "This is it, isn't it? The source of the thing that's controlling you."

"Nothing is controlling me," Henry said, trying to shake off the effects of the mystical jolt mixing with the early onset of shock and blood loss. "You need to stop. You don't understand what you're doing."

"I'm setting you free, Henry," Don said, pressing the blade into the flesh inside the circle and then slicing down, breaking the inked boundary.

Henry screamed.

Lexie walked into the vestibule of Henry's building, looking around for the doorman and trying to catch her breath. She'd sprinted since she left the cab but stopped when she'd gotten to his block, not wanting to look like a completely winded psychopath when she got there. The doorman, a turtle-shaped middle aged man with a mop of curly hair covered by a poorly fitting hat, was sitting at a desk off to the side of the door watching football on a small TV.

"How's it goin'?" He asked, getting to his feet and walking over.

"Hey," she said. "Randy, right? I'm Lexie, I work with Mr. Churchill, up on four. Did he have any visitors today? Are they still here?"

Randy stopped, looking Lexie up and down. "I'm not sure he'd appreciate me telling folks about his visitors."

Lexie nodded. "Okay, fair enough. Can you buzz him and let him know I'm here? It's important."

Randy nodded. "Alright. Sure." He walked back over to the switchboard by his desk and touched one of the buttons. They waited, Lexie tapping her feet on the polished stone floor. Randy pushed it again. More waiting.

"They're still up there, right?" She asked. Randy nodded, pushing the button a third time. "And their visitor is still up there too, right? Older guy, in his fifties. Balding a little, salt and pepper hair, kinda burly?"

"What's this about, Miss?"

"Nothing good, Randy," she said, heading for the elevators. "I'm going up. If I don't come down you're going to have some problems on your hands."

"Whatever you say, lady," Randy muttered, going back to his desk.

In the elevator, Lexie took several deep breaths. Even if Don was still there it wasn't a certainty that he was going to be violent. He may be just trying to get some sort of dirt on Henry or find some evidence of his crazy "possession" theory. She'd have to come clean with him about how she'd gone behind his back but she'd was going to own up to that anyway.

The important thing, she told herself as she left the elevator, was to not go in there all guns blazing and making a scene. Be calm, be rational, and be honest. There was no need for craziness.

She turned the corner, heard the screaming from Henry's apartment and started running.

As soon as the blade broke the circle Henry could feel the thing inside him uncoiling like a snake. The pain it felt at Don's hands was forgotten as it began to surge through his body, mind and soul.

Don jerked back, tipping over the chair he'd been sitting on and stumbling to remain on his feet. The blade he'd been cutting with dropped onto the plastic, the tip landing in a pile of congealing blood and sizzling like a hot pan dropped in cold water.

Henry thrashed, the strength he'd thought he'd lost now surging through him. Everything was clearer now. He just had to force himself free, grab the blade and plunge it deep into Don's neck. That might be too quick, he realized. There are plenty of other things he could use to make him suffer.

Henry closed his eyes and forced his body to remain

still. He began to recite a spell under his breath to try to regain his control.

"Begone demon! By the power of the Lord I command you to get thee hence!" Don yelled.

Henry could feel the waves of Don's energy coursing over him. It burned and he could feel the demon inside him pushing back against it.

"Shut the fuck up, Don," Henry said, opening his eyes and glaring at him. Don's power fluttered and Henry knew Don wouldn't have a chance to banish this thing. All he was going to do was draw it out before Henry could get it back under control.

Don cleared his throat and stepped forward again, raising a hand high and trying to regain his composure. Henry gathered a mouthful of spit and spat it into Don's eye. Don recoiled screaming as the spit hissed and sizzled, burning him.

Henry clamped his mouth shut, teeth sharper than they should be biting into his lip. There was a pounding, and he couldn't tell if it was from inside his head or out, but he tried to block it out and recited the spell in his head again.

He felt the pounding in his chest intensify the more the spell repeated over and over in his mind. His head and chest were burning from the inside out and he felt his stomach churning violently.

Jailor. We meet again, so soon after the last time.

Henry bore down, repeating the spell again.

Not again. Never again, mortal filth.

Henry screamed as he felt his insides burn.

Lexie pounded on the door as hard as she could. "Henry! Henry!" The scream hadn't been his but she got less sure of that by the second.

She pounded on the door again, her fist stinging from the force of it. She gave it another second before stepping back and kicking the door just above the knob. The door opened with a crack from the door frame and then bounced back from the chain. Lexie lowered her shoulder and rammed it, wincing as a shower of wood splinters peppered her face as she burst through.

Don was sitting on the floor, a hand up to his left eye, blood seeping through the fingers. In the center of the room Henry sat tied to a large, high backed chair. His normally crisp white shirt torn to tatters and the skin under it and on the tops of his thighs were cut and slashed and there were at least six silver handled needles stuck in him, including one through the top of his hand.

Henry thrashed in the chair and Lexie moved to help him until he looked over at her, freezing her in place. There was blood dripping down his chin and onto his lap. He was growling and his eyes were bloody, tears of red beginning to run down his face, and his pupils were flattened and elongated vertically like a snakes.

The only time she'd seen anything like this was the spell she watched Henry try. She'd re-watched the footage multiple times before sending it to Don but she didn't remember it being this violent. The protection circle he'd been in must've kept the waves of power radiating off of him at bay because she didn't remember the primal fear and terror boiling inside of her then like they were now. She closed her eyes, concentrating on standing her ground and not running in abject terror.

"See?" Don said, getting to his feet and gesturing at Henry. "I was right! I told you I wa--"

She spun and punched him so hard she could the bones in his nose crumble under her fist. He staggered back, falling to one knee. She kicked him across the face and he flipped over and stopped moving. She turned her attention back to Henry, who was thrashing and growling more now, the waves of energy coming off of him making her insides twitch. As he twisted and writhed around in the chair one of its arms snapped off, leaving it dangling from the plastic zip tie wrapped around his wrist. With his free hand began scratching and clawing at the belt tied around his chest, doing more damage to himself than it.

"Henry!" she shouted, walking towards him with open hands out and stopping just before she reached the tarp. "It's Lexie. You've got to stop this, okay? Pull it together and just...stop, alright?"

He stared at her, growling settling in to a low rumble as he appraised her from top to bottom with his blood-filled lizard eyes. "Henry, please. Let me help you."

He spat up a massive wad of blood and mucus that hit the tarp with a splash that almost reached her shoes. He let out a roar that echoed with noises that shouldn't be able to be made by the human throat. Underneath it she could hear a rhythmic voice that seemed to be repeating a series of words over and over again. Henry's head writhed around, mouth still open and sounds rising in volume until it was so loud she had to cover her ears. There was an electrical snap and a fountain of black gore spewed out of Henry's mouth. As it splashed on the ground a wave of force slammed into her, knocking her on to her back.

She pushed herself up and saw that Henry was now limp in his chair, eyes fluttering and head lolling to the side. She went to stand but stopped when she felt that invisible force pushing her back down. She crawled along the floor away from Henry involuntarily, her hands trembling. "Henry!" she screamed, her voice trembling. "Wake up!" Henry lifted his head and opened his eyes. She could see that the sharp teeth and lizard eyes he'd had before we gone.

In the pile of gore and blood on the tarp in front of Henry something was stirring. Bits of it began to rise up and then trickle slowly back down. Lexie tried to stand but could only keep subconsciously pushing herself further away from what Henry had thrown up. It was stretching and rising up out of the blood but hazy like a mirage, giving it an indistinct shape. It was tall, reaching almost to the ceiling and stretching out across the room like an insect unfolding multi-jointed limbs. She opened her mouth to call out for Henry but stopped when she felt the thing turning towards her.

A chant started and she looked past the demonic thing to see Henry, fully awake now, raising his free hand above his head. It was shaking but a glow began to spread over it, energy arcing between his fingers. The thing in the room spun around and Henry winced, stuttering one of the words and causing the power in his hand to flicker. The thing advanced but Henry bore down, restarting the chant, louder this time.

The demon shrieked, a sound that shook Lexie down to her bones, and Henry's voice rose and a sudden burst of energy exploded from his hand. The bits of blood and bile giving the thing shape collapsed to the ground and the force of its presence lifted immediately. Henry's hand fell down into his lap and his head sagged to the side. She scrambled over to him, trying to step gingerly on the tarp so that she didn't slip and fall.

"Henry, wake up. C'mon, man." She patted his face gently and he grunted in annoyance.

"I'm sorry," she said. "I'm so, so sorry." She looked him over, not sure where to start but figured that the needles sticking out of him were as good a place as any. "This is going to hurt," she said, grabbing at one sticking out of the top of his

153

thigh and yanking it out. A small dot of blood formed and trickled off to the side. She pulled the rest out quickly and dabbed at the dots of blood with a scrap of Henry's shirt, thankful that it seemed like Don hadn't hit any major arteries.

She slid the broken arm out from the tie at his wrist but the one around his other wrist was fastened too tight, as were the ones on his ankles. The belt around his chest looked easy enough to undo but she wanted to be sure he could hold himself up. "Hold on, okay?" she said.

She ran to the kitchen and began pulling open drawers until she found a large serrated knife. She darted back and began to saw through the tie on his wrist. It took some doing and ended up taking a couple of bits of wood with it.

"Sorry," she said, kneeling down to start on the ones around his ankles. "But in my defense you ruined the chair first." Henry groaned a little, free hand dropping limply in his lap.

"Nothing?" She said, sawing away. "Give me something here, Henry or I'll just leave you and start on that turkey in the oven. It looks delicious."

Henry groaned again, eyes fluttering. "There we go," she said, the first tie snapping. "Where are Monica and the kids, Henry? Talk to me."

Henry murmured something as she massaged the circulation back into his foot. "Come on, mumbles. Speak up."

"Don't know," he said. "He said they were fine."

"He better pray they are," she said starting on the last tie. "One more, okay? Then I'm gonna go get you cleaned up and look for them."

"No," he said, his voice trailing off again. "Get out. Get them out."

"No one is going anywhere until you're fixed up." She sawed at the tie. "I don't know if you noticed you're kind of in a bad way."

He gave a little chuckle that trailed off into a rasping cough. "It doesn't matter. Get them and go."

"You're being stupid," she said, finishing cutting the tie and getting to her feet. "I'm already pissed off, don't add to it by saying dumb shit." She unbuckled the belt across his chest and he wobbled but managed to keep himself upright.

"Come on," she said, lifting him to his feet and putting his arm over her shoulder. "I'm gonna get you into the bathroom and see what we can do about these cuts. You're bleeding all over an outfit I actually put thought in to."

He let out a grunting noise that sounded like he was in pain but after a couple of steps she realized he was laughing. "Wow, that's funny to you? Geez, way to thank the lady who untied you from a chair."

"It's a little funny," he mumbled.

"Alright smart ass," she said easing him into the hallway. "Let's see how funny you think things are when I dump a bottle of hydrogen peroxide all over you."

"Just leave me," he said. "You need to find them and go."

Before she could say anything Lexie looked into the open door of Henry and Monica's bedroom. Monica, John and Lilly were laying on the bed, all three had their wrists and ankles tied with zip ties. Their mouths were gagged but their eyes were closed. Lexie stopped watching to make sure all three were taking breaths before she nudged Henry with her hip.

"They are safe," she said. "Look."

Henry raised his head and let out a choked sound of relief. "Okay. Just put me down and then get them out of here."

"I will put you down," she said, continuing towards the bathroom, "and then take care of them but we're all going to be safe, okay?"

Henry shook his head. "No, not safe. Never safe."

"Well, yeah. That's life, buddy," she said, dragging him into the bathroom. "I'm gonna set you down in the tub so you don't bleed all over the place. Well, more all over the place."

Henry gave a weak nod. "You need to get them out of here. Promise me."

"Hey," she said, lifting his head to look into his eyes. She could see that the tracks of blood that had run down his face were being washed away by slow, heavy tears. "I promise you that they won't be hurt. You have my word."

Henry opened his mouth to say something and then just nodded. She eased him down into the tub, both of them wincing as she tried to find a grip on him that wasn't a tattered shirt or skin slick with blood. She grabbed the towels off the rack and handed them to him. "I hope these aren't the good towels." He shook his head with a weak smile.

"I'll be right back, okay? Just try to stop some of the bleeding."

Henry shook his head. "Lexie, please. It's still not safe." She was about to brush him off again but now that she could see his face clearly she could tell this was more than just concern about what Don had done to him.

"Henry, how bad is it?"

He cringed as he dabbled the towels on the cuts that were still seeping blood. "Very bad, and we're not done yet. When you get Monica tell her I said 'Westwood.'"

"Westwood?"

"Yes. Now go, I don't know how much time we have left."

"I called Harmony to be on standby in case I didn't check in. Should I have her come help?"

Henry shook his head vigorously. "No. This is my mess. I'll clean it up. I don't want any else in danger."

Harmony nodded and as she headed back to the bedroom she took out her phone and dialed Harmony.

"You're really cutting it close babe. Like, three minutes close. What's going on?"

"It's bad. I think we took care of it but I was right.

157

When I got here Don had Henry tied to a chair and was torturing him."

"Fuck's sake. Is he okay? Do you need me?"

"No. Can you just make up some excuse for me and try to have a good time without me?"

"Yes to the first and probably not to the second. Are you sure you're alright? You don't sound good."

"It's okay," she said, closing her eyes and seeing the thing that had come out of Henry. "I'll let you know when I'm home."

"Alright. I...just be safe, okay?"

"I will."

She hung up and shot off a text to Martin saying Henry was out of danger and that she would call later. She tucked her phone away and went into the living room to retrieve the knife she'd used to cut Henry free. When she saw Don still laying on the ground she picked up the belt he'd strapped Henry to the chair and walked over to him.

She rolled him over on his side, took the belt and wrapped it around his right wrist a couple of times before bending his left leg back and tying the other end of the belt to it. She tested it to make sure sure he wouldn't be able to break out of it and then headed back to the bedroom, resisting the urge to kick him again on the way.

All three of them were still out, but Monica was twitching like someone having a bad dream. Lexie untied the gags around their mouths and then slipped the blade of the knife between Monica's wrists and cut the tie. She rolled over moaning but keeping her eyes closed. Lexie freed her ankles and then cut the kids loose.

"Monica," she said, giving her a gentle shake. "Monica, I need you to get up." She rolled over, eyes fluttering. "Come on, Monica. Henry needs you." She groaned a little but her eyes stayed shut.

"Lexie!" Henry yelled from the bathroom. "What's going on? Are they okay?"

"I'm just trying to wake them up, alright?" She yelled back. The yell caused all three of them to sitr and Lexie grabbed Monica's shoulder and shook it harder this time. "Monica, you've got to wake up and get your husband off my back, okay?"

Her eyes opened more this time. "Henry?" She muttered.

"He's okay," she said. "But you've gotta get up." Monica shook her head again, trying to sit up in the bed. "The kids? Are they--" she stopped when she felt them laying next to her. "Oh thank god," she said, reaching out and touching them as if she didn't think they were actually there. "Where's Henry?" She said, her eyes widening when she saw the blood smeared on Lexie's shirt and pants.

"He's okay," Lexie said and Monica let out a sigh of relief. "Well, he's not great but he's going to be okay."

"Where is he?"

"He's in the bathroom and kind of freaking out a little. He told me to tell you 'Westwood.' Does that--"

Monica turned and took John and Lilly each by the shoulder, shaking them furiously. "Kids! Get up! C'mon now!" The two groaned and began to roll around.

"I mean it, get up now!" In a sharp, Angry Mom voice, which got them sitting up, eyes fluttering open. John realized what had happened first but Lilly followed quickly after.

"Mom oh god what--"

"What happened did--"

"Stop!" Monica said, putting a hand up and silencing them both. "I need you both to listen to me. Something has happened and I need you to do what I say, is that clear?"

They both nodded and looked over at Lexie for the first time. Both sets of eyes went wide when they saw Lexie and the blood on her clothes. "Hey," she said, giving a little wave and then regretting it. "It's okay, you're safe now." Monica glared at her and then motioned towards the closet.

"Lexie, can I get your help over here?"

Lexie nodded and followed her. Monica went right into the closet and pushed aside the mass of Henry's dress shirts that hung there like jungle foliage. "Push on that wall there," Monica said, holding back the tide of shirts.

It took a couple of tries but when Lexie pushed in the right spot the wall swung out to reveal a small room behind it.

It was about five foot square with a small set of shelves in the back stocked with many trinkets, charms and other paraphernalia that she recognized from the storage closet at the office. Painted onto the wood floor was one of Henry's protection circles.

"Come on," Monica said, waving for the kids to get in there. They hopped off the bed and approached the small room cautiously. "Go on, hurry," Monica said, herding them into the middle of the circle. There was just enough room for the two of them to sit and leave just enough for a couple of people to stand.

"Hold it open," Monica said, walking in and going for the small safe in the back corner. She typed in the combination and opened it. Inside were a pair of pistols, both .45 revolvers, and what looked to be an old combat knife. Monica took a pistol and gave the other to Lexie.

"Stay with them," Monica said, heading back out to the bedroom. "The door locks from the inside and should keep almost anything out. If you hear anything close it until you get the all clear."

"Monica," Lexie was stopped by Monica's raised finger.

"I am going to get my husband. I'm not just going to leave him hurt and bleeding while I take our children and hide. Now please, stay here and make sure nothing happens to them. Can you do that?"

Lexie looked down at the revolver, opened the chamber to make sure it was loaded and then snapped it back into place. "Yes ma'am."

Monica nodded, her expression softening. She looked back at the kids and managed a smile for them. "It'll be okay," she said, before turning and heading out of the room.

Lexie turned and nodded at them, moving a little into the safe room enough that she could both keep an eye on the entrance to the bedroom and pull the door closed. The two just stared up at her.

"Holidays are the worst, am I right?" " She finally said. " It elicited a small chuckle from John but Lilly just stared at her.

"Your mom was right," Lexie said. "Everything is going to be fine."

"Jesus Christ, Henry," Monica said when she came in the bathroom. He'd pulled himself out of the bathtub and was now sitting on its edge. He'd gotten his pants and shirt off and had begun tearing them into strips to wrap around the cuts that were still seeping blood.

"I thought I told Lexie to get you and the kids out of here. I gave her the emergency word."

"Screw your emergency word and screw you for thinking I was going to leave you behind. She and the kids are in the safe room. I gave up a walk in closet for it the least we can do is actually use it when there's trouble." She sat down in front of him, putting the pistol on the ground and taking the strip of shirt he'd been about to use from his hand.

"Do you still remember how to use that?" He said, wincing as she wrapped it around his thigh and tightened it.

"You know that I do," she said, looking him over. "What did he..." She trailed off when she saw the cut across the circle tattooed on his chest. "Oh my god. You said that if the circle ever broke--"

"That it'd take me over? It almost did. I was able to push it out before that happened."

"So that's it? It's finally gone?"

Henry shook his head. "No. That's why I was trying to get you and the kids out. It's loose and getting more powerful by the moment, and I don't think I'm strong enough to stop it."

He could see them burning. Everything in the world, burning and screaming. Masses of people were before him, pleading and begging for mercy and it struck him how similar it was to when he used to preach. This time, however, instead of looking up at him with wide, dull cow eyes they were looking with fear and pain.

Don opened his eyes and the vision faded away. He winced in pain, first when he tried to breathe through his broken nose but followed quickly by the searing ache in his left eye.

He tried to get up but was off balance. He closed his right eye and everything went dark. He tried to close his left but even trying to move that side of his face sent a fresh charge of pain through him. He rolled over and then realized why he was so off balance. His right hand had been tied to his left foot and all he was doing was rolling on the ground like a beached fish.

He opened his mouth to yell for Lexie and Henry but he realized he wasn't alone. He couldn't see it but he could feel it, like someone standing behind him. He turned around as much as his awkward position would allow and could feel something getting closer.

He pushed himself up with his free arm and tried to get a better look at his surroundings but his damaged eye made that difficult. He looked around the room and then he saw it, indistinct and blurry, stretching to the ceiling with long, multi-jointed limbs that ended in sharp, terrible things. It was straddling him with its legs and dropping down on him.

He tried to pull himself away with his free arm but the burning electric force he'd felt before was pressing down on him. Don thrashed, trying to work his way out from under it but it intensified, sending shocks all through his body. The burning in his ruined eye magnified and he opened his mouth to scream. Before any sound came out the thing pushed Don's head down and he could feel it pushing down his throat, a searing electrical heat throbbing in its wake.

He could see them in his mind again, the screaming,

burning masses and he realized they weren't screaming in fear of him but the thing wearing Don like an ill fitting suit, its horns, claws, and wings bursting out of his body.

That's when it allowed him to scream.

Henry struggled to his feet wincing in pain and making his way to the bathroom door. He motioned for Monica to hand him the pistol and after he checked the safety he leaned out into the hall. The only thing he saw was Lexie at the other end of the hall peering out as well.

She looked quizzically at him and he nodded that he and Monica were okay. She indicated towards the archway across the hall from her that led into the dining and living rooms and he nodded. He motioned towards the door to John's room, across the hall from him and she nodded again.

"What's happening?" Monica asked in a whisper. "Are the kids--"

"They're fine. Stay here, Lex and I are going to check it out." He looked back out at Lexie, who gave him a three count and then the two of them moved together, her to the archway leading in to the living room and him to the doorway to John's room.

Lexie leaned into the living room and then came right back. She looked back at him and shook her head. Henry left the doorway and moved up the hallway stopping right next to her.

"Anything?"

"I can't really see anything. Whatever it was it came from the living room, but it sure didn't sound like Don."

"He's the least of our problems."

"What is it?" Monica said, coming up behind Henry.

"We don't know," he said. "You should be in the safe room. Or at least make sure the kids stay in there."

She glared at him and then darted back to the bedroom door. They could hear her reassure them until the door of the room muffled their noises.

"I hope I'm wrong but I'm guessing that big, barely in this reality thing you puked up that nearly made me piss myself didn't get destroyed when you did your whole 'get thee hence' magic, huh?"

Henry shook his head.

"Fan-tastic," Lexie said. "Well, we knew this job was dangerous when we took it, right?"

"Something like that," Henry said. "Ready?"

"On three," she said. They nodded off three silent beats and then rushed into the living room. All that was waiting for them was the broken chair still in the center of the plastic, blood stained tarp. Don had disappeared and the belt she'd bound his hand and foot with lay on the ground in two pieces, the leather pulled apart and frayed.

"That's not good," Lexie said, looking over at the door to the apartment, which stood ajar. The splintered wood of the frame around the lock kept it from closing all the way.

"No, it isn't."

"Did that thing...did it eat Don or what?"

Henry ran a hand over the thin covering of hair on his head. "No, it took him. Possessed him, probably."

"One point for irony then. So he's gone?"

Henry walked to the open door and peered out into the hallway. It was quiet and empty. He closed the door as much as he could, pushing it enough so that the doorknob lock clicked into place as much as the broken wood allowed. It wasn't secure but it kept the door from hanging open and was hopefully inconspicuous enough from the other side.

"Sorry,"Lexie said. "But I will point out I almost arrived in time to stop all this."

Henry nodded, leaning against the wall. His body was still store and coming down from the sudden wave of panic made him light headed. "It's alright. The door is shielded from demonic spirits and magic but it it only works if it's intact."

"Fuck. What about everyone else in the building?"

"Same on their doors. As long as people keep them closed then they're safe. The front of the building too."

"So it's trapped in here with us?"

He nodded, pushing off from the wall and wobbling slightly. "For now. It's weak and still recovering. Soon it'll be either be able to break through the barriers on its own or be strong enough to call for help."

"Help? Shit, we've got help of our own. I can get Harmony and Martin down here with whatever you need from the office--"

"No! No one else! My family is already in danger because of me and I'm not going to risk anyone else!"

Lexie took a deep breath. "So just us, then?"

"Yeah, but more me than you. I can draw it back into me and trap it but--"

"Wait, how is that a solution? Let's just destroy it while its weak, right?"

"We can't, trust me this is the only way."

"No, I can't accept that. You being possessed again by this thing just--"

"I was not possessed!" He snapped. "I know that's what you and Don thought but, surprisingly, it's more complicated than that! This thing is only here because I summoned him when I was young and stupid and the only way to fix it was to trap it inside me and for twenty years things were fine! So maybe, instead of doubting me because I didn't share the biggest, most shameful secret with someone I barely know you trust that I know what I'm talking about. Can you do that?"

Lexie nodded, looking down at the floor. "Yeah, sure. Can you do me a favor?"

"What?"

"Can you put some pants on? It's hard to take you seriously and feel properly shitty about this when you're in your boxers."

"Goddammit," he chuckled, heading back towards the bedroom. "Come on, I've got to get other stuff from the safe room."

"All I can say is thank god for the button fly," she said following after him. Just as they got to the door to the bedroom she reached out and put a hand on his shoulder. "Look, I'm really sorry, okay? I didn't think anything like this would happen."

"I know. We can work it out later. Let's just make sure no one else gets hurt."

"Sure," she said following him and the pulling up suddenly. "Shit! The doorman!"

"Randy? I thought he said he wasn't working today."

"Well he is. What should we do?"

"Go down there and get him out of the building and lock it up."

"What're you going to do?"

"I can start working the ritual to draw him back in but it's going to take some time."

"And if I run into Don?"

Henry thought about it for a second. "Do what you need to do. I'd say shoot to kill but the demon may be too powerful for that now. Do whatever you can to keep him from leaving. The seals on the building are slowing the return of its power but it's only a matter of time before it's at full strength."

Lexie nodded. "Can do."

"Just be careful, okay? And make sure the door latches behind you when you go."

She nodded and took off. He went in the bedroom and grabbed a pair of pants and a tee shirt and slipped them on. He went to the closed door of the safe room and tapped four quick knocks. "Wildwood, honey. It's me."

The lock clicked and the door slid open. "Is it--" she started but stopped when she saw the look on his face.

"Daddy!" Lilly said leaping to her feet, rushing forward and embracing him, eliciting a pained wince. John got to his feet as well, looking at his father with a mixture of relief and terror.

"Dad what's going on?" he said.

"It's okay, we're going to be fine," Henry said to Lilly, patting her on the head as he tried to pull away from her painfully tight grip. "I mean it, everything is fine."

"Fine?" John said. "Dad, we were drugged and now we're hiding in a room full of Satan stuff!"

Lilly looked up at him, tears running down her cheeks. "Daddy I don't want to be a Satanist."

"We're not Satanists," he said. "We're the opposite. All of this stuff is to fight evil and this room is going to keep you safe, okay? I just need to get a few things and stay in here a little while longer, okay?"

Lily let go and nodded at him. John stared at him, jaw

set in anger, but he nodded and sat back down. Henry squeezed into the room and took a couple of medallions from one of the small shelves and a small leather bound book from a small row of books from the opposite side.

"I'll be back and then all of this will be over, okay?" The kids nodded at him and he turned and left, the lie burning on his lips.

After making sure the hallway was clear, Lexie raced towards the stairwell. She pushed the door open a crack to see if she could see or hear anything but it was just as quiet as the hallway. She headed down, taking the stairs two at a time and pausing at each landing to make sure nothing was waiting for her.

When she made it to the first floor she eased the door open to listen for it. She could hear Randy talking to someone and she hurried down the hall, pistol held out of sight behind her on the off chance this was a visiting Grandmother running late for dinner.

"Sir, I said are you okay?" She heard Randy say as she reached the entryway to the building. She peered around the corner and saw Don staring at the closed doors leading out of the building. He was still wearing blood covered surgical gloves and seemed completely oblivious to Randy's presence.

"Sir, I said--" Randy stopped as Don raised a blood covered hand towards the door. It got close to it, about six inches or so, before it began to tremble as if it was exerting itself as hard as it could pushing against some kind of invisible force. Randy, just noticing the blood on the man's hands, opened his mouth and then closed it.

He was on the opposite side of Don's ruined eye, Harmony realized. "Hey," she called to him, trying to keep her voice low enough that Don wouldn't notice her. "Randy, hey!"

He glanced over at her and then pointed at Don. "Hey, this guy needs help!"

"Fuck's sake, Randy get over here! That guy is crazy!"

Randy took a step towards her, head tilted in a confused simpleton kind of way. "What are you..." He looked back over Don, who was turning his attention from the doors and to Randy. He looked over and as Don turned his head his burned, blood-seeping eye and smashed, bloody nose came into view.

"Jesus," Randy whispered, taking a step back from him. "This guy really needs help."

"Dammit Randy," she said, coming out from cover and raising the pistol. "Get away from him, that guy is seriously dangerous."

"Are yo--" Don darted forward, hand wrapping around Randy's throat. In two quick steps Don dragged Randy backwards and then slammed him against the wall. The doorman's eyes rolled back and his head fell to the side, revealing a red smear where his skull hit the shiny marble wall.

"The door," Don growled. "Open it." His voice was still Don's but there was an echo to it that made her flinch.

"Not a chance," she said, stepping forward and taking careful aim with the pistol.

"He's still alive. Open the door and I'll let him live."

"I open the door you'll kill a lot more." She said, stepping closer. There was only about six feet between them now and given how fast he moved before, she wondered if she'd be able to get any shots off before he could grab her.

"Fine," it said. "Then this one doesn't matter." He swung his free hand up into Randy's skull, punching right through it with a shower of bone and flesh and cracking the stone behind him. He dropped Randy's mostly headless body to the ground and she fired three shots, falling back as fast as she could.

Don ducked around her bullets and then he was in front of her, clamping a hand down on the pistol. She let go just as he yanked it out of her hand and sent it flying. She fell backwards as his hand grabbed for her, hitting the ground and rolling away as his fist crashed down where she'd been.

She sprung to her feet, heading for the door to the stairs. She kicked the wooden doorstop out and swung the door shut and kept running. She didn't look back to see if latched before Don got to it but she heard it crash into the wall with such force that the sound of it echoed all around her. The door to the stairs was closed and she was only a foot away from it when she Don's voice roared at her from behind. She couldn't even make out the words as the force of them lifted her off her feet and slammed her into the door ahead of her, bouncing off it and landing on her back. She rolled over, coughing and trying to get air back into her lungs, unsure if it was the impact or the things voice that drove it out of her. She pushed herself up on all fours and reached for the door handle, but before her fingers could close around it, a hand grabbed her ankle and she was yanked away. Her head bounced against the floor and the world swam in front of her as Don dragged her through the hallway and back into the building's vestibule. She kicked at him with her free leg but it didn't faze him at all.

"Willing or not, you will set me free," Don said, stopping a few feet in front of the double doors leading outside. She pushed herself up with her hands, trying to get close enough to push free of his grip but then she was airborne as he swung her into the doors by her ankle. She slammed into them and felt them buckle with the impact.

She dropped the ground in front of them, gasping in pain. "It's a pull," she croaked, the words sending ripples of pain down her back. Don snarled and kicked at her. She flinched back, realizing this may have been what her Dad meant when he'd said her smart mouth would get her in real trouble one day and that he'd probably greet her in the afterlife with an "I told you so."

Through a half closed eye she saw Don's foot stop a

couple of inches from her face. He stepped back and kicked again but with the same result. She got to her feet, keeping her back flush against the door.

Don stepped closer but the barrier kept him about three inches from her face. "Looks like Henry built these barriers to last," she smirked. Don sneered and then roared at her, mouth opening impossibly wide as the nearly . She felt the air rush towards her and the cavernous sound of it but it had none of the physical force it had before.

"Throwing a tantrum isn't going to help anything, Don."

"Fine. Maybe this will," Don said, grabbing Randy's small desk.

"Ah, fuck," she said as he swung it at her.

The spell was more complicated than Henry remembered, but he preferred to chalk that up to the torture and not the twenty years of age since he last performed it. As the energy built up around him he could feel the world falling away. He closed his eyes, the words of the spell now etched in his mind. He took one of the medallions and wrapped it around his right wrist. His hand began to tremble and he balled it into a fist, steadying himself. He said the words of the spell again, carefully wrapping the other medallion around his left wrist with a shaking hand. Once it was wrapped tight the uncontrollable flutter moved from his hands and into his chest.

He remembered this part. It scared the shit out of him when he was younger and he remembered thinking *I don't want to die like this.* Twenty three years later, he thought *I don't want to die, but if it's like this at least it'll mean something.*

Before he'd started the spell he'd collected a small cup of his blood and now he dipped his finger in it and began to draw a containment circle on his chest. The palpitations of his his heart grew more erratic but he fought through them.

Not yet. Not just yet.

His heartbeat went from unpredictable flutter to rapid-fire explosions, as if there was a vice around his heart and it was trying to break free. It grew in intensity with every line he drew, reaching a triple time crescendo and stopped as soon as he took his finger off of his chest. Henry gasped and fell backwards. His vision went gray and the whole world faded away from him. He was falling, aware on that he was leaving his body behind.

Okay. Now we can go.

Lexie ducked down and slid to the side, the desk hitting where she'd been standing. It splintered, the cheap pressed wood and thin metal yielding to the solid door. Don lifted the remains up and slammed it down at her. She scrambled away in the only direction she had, away from the doors and out into the vestibule. Don hurled the remains of desk at her and she ducked under it, diving towards him. As fast and as strong as he was she knew the only chance she had, even if it was ridiculously slim, was up close.

He swung a fist down at her but she rolled behind him and leapt up, wrapping a leg around his and circling an arm around his neck, grasping as tight as she could while he thrashed around a wild animal. It took a couple of tries to pull herself fully onto his back and wrap her free leg around his torso. She pulled and twisted with her arms, but whatever demonic strength Don was channeling, it was enough to keep her from being able to break his neck.

Don screamed, the force it directed at the ground as he pitched forward, trying to throw her off of him. She dug in with her legs and kept herself on his back like a giant toddler. For a second she imagined how ridiculous they must look from outside, his arms reaching back to grab at her as she clung to him as close as she could. *Don't mind us, it's just our traditional Thanksgiving Violent Piggyback Ride.* She tightened her grip around his throat, switching from twisting his neck to trying to crush his throat. Hopefully the demon hadn't taken away his need to breathe.

She squeezed as hard as she could and Don stopped moving, leaning forward until he was bent at a ninety degree angle. "There we go," she said. "Nighty ni--" and then they were airborne, flying up so high she swore she could feel one of the hanging light fixtures brush past her head before they arced back down, Don's weight crashing on top of her as her back hit the lobby floor.

"Oh fuck you," she gasped. There was a sudden stabbing pain in her torso and she knew she'd cracked at least a couple of ribs. Her grip around his neck loosened with the impact and he was thrashing and squirming again, trying to pull away. Her hand came free but her arm was still around his neck. She punched the side of his head with her free hand but with no effect. The thrashing stopped and he dug his feet into the floor and pressed down on her. Air rushed out of her and she felt the strain not just in her already injured ribs but neck and shoulders, Don's unnatural strength threatening to grind her bones like powder.

She unwrapped her legs from his, trying to push out from under him but she was completely pinned. She kept her arm wrapped around his neck, hoping she'd be able to squeeze the air out of him before bones started breaking, but the angle was no good now.

She reached back with her free hand, hoping to find something to either help pull her out from under him or something to use as a weapon. She found a piece of the metal frame of the desk and turned it around so the flattened end with a screw still hanging loosely from it was pointed down at Don. She stabbed down, getting him on the side of the face with the ruined eye, the end of the metal digging into his cheek and eye over and over again until she felt blood and humor splash up on her hand. He flinched away but gave no other sign of discomfort and didn't show any signs of letting her slip away.

178

A bright light descended from the ceiling and she thought for a moment that she was going to meet her end in a way she never thought possible, crushed to death under some guy, but the swirling mass of blue-green light dropped onto Don, enveloping the both of them in a warm glow.

Don doubled over, taking the pressure off of Lexie. She let go of his neck and kicked him away, rolling onto her side and drawing in breath in deep gasps that made her ribs flare with pain in protest. The glow around him pulsed from blue to red to orange and was so bright Lexie couldn't look directly at it. The was a white flash and then it flew back up through the ceiling, leaving a flickering afterimage in her eyes and Don sprawled on the floor.

Lexie got to her feet and walked over to him. He was on his back, arms and legs akimbo. There was a loose flap of skin on his cheek and his eye, which had already been burned, was now a soggy, gaping hole. She almost checked to see if he was alive but he took a shallow breath and let out a small moan of pain that trailed off into a weak sob.

"Good enough," she said, trotting over to where the pistol had been tossed, grabbing it and then heading for the elevator. The ride up felt like it took forever but she knew if she tried running up the steps her body would be screaming in pain by the time she got up there. She tucked the pistol in the waistband of her pants and when the elevator doors opened she hurried down the hall as fast as she could without running, although trying not to attract attention at this point seemed a little pointless.

She put an ear to Henry's door and took the pistol out. She couldn't hear anything so she opened the door, pistol up and ready for whatever demonic force flew out at her. There was nothing, just Henry laying on his back, arms and legs spread just like Don in the lobby below.

"Henry?" She said, and then she realized he wasn't breathing.

"Goddammit," she said, tucking the pistol back into her pants and running to his side. She put an ear to his chest and heard nothing. She tilted his head back and began CPR, wincing at the metallic taste of blood on his mouth. She compressed his chest carefully, hoping that it wouldn't affect the symbols he'd painted there.

"C'mon Henry," muttered between compressions. "You're a tough son of a bitch. Don't make all this for nothing."

She breathed into him again and compressed his chest harder this time. "Come on, wake up you stubborn bas--"

He took a giant breath, chest rising off the plastic. His eyes opened and she could see them swimming with blood, which began to run down his face like tears. She leaned away, drawing the pistol and pointing it at him. He sat up, faster than she thought he'd be capable of grabbing her wrist painfully and pushing the gun away from him. She tried to budge it back but he was too strong.

"It's okay," he said. "You can stop now, I'm fine."

"You sure?"

"Not really, seeing as how I've been tortured, my family terrified and had to perform magic that nearly killed me."

"Right," she said, standing up and offering a hand to help him up. He took it and pulled himself to his feet with a wince of pain. "Sorry about that. Well, about everything really."

"I know," he said, taking a step and then wobbling. She took his shoulders and guided him over to the sofa. He dropped into it with another wince of pain. "Is Don..."

"He's alive. A bit worse for wear but alive. Is this done? Are we good?"

Henry chuckled. "It's never done, Lexie. And I'll never be 'good,' since that thing is trapped inside me again but yes, for now we are safe. Can you go get my family and then maybe call for an ambulance?" He leaned his head back and closed his eyes, taking a long deep breath.

"Sure thing," she said, waiting a moment to make sure his breathing was steady before heading to the safe room.

"You have got to be kidding me." Lexie said when Henry walked into the office. It was the Tuesday after Thanksgiving and Monica had said he was going to stay home at least another week.

"What am I going to do, hang around the house all day?" He said, limping over to his desk and putting his coat and hat up.

"Yes, generally that's what recovering entails."

He sat down as slow as he could but could still feel some of the stitches tugging painfully at his skin. "I can recover here, besides we--"

"Holy shit!" Martin said, pulling up short as he stepped into the office, nearly spilling the tray of coffees he was carrying. "You're back! Lexie said it'd be a week or so before you came back."

"That's what I thought," she said. "But Dr. Churchill here figured otherwise."

"No kidding. Henry, do you want me to get you a coffee or something? No problem at all, man. Whatever you need."

Henry nodded. "That'd be great. When you get back can you give Lexie and I a minute? I'll come out and get it."

Lexie sighed and Martin looked from her to him. "Sure thing. Let me know when you're ready." He backed out of the room, closing the door behind him. When they heard the outer door of the office close Lexie got to her feet.

"Look, if you're going to fire me I'd rather not have a whole lecture. I know I fucked up but--"

"You're not fired," he said, waving for her to sit back down.

"Are you sure? Because I'd fire me."

"Since you didn't tie me to a chair and start cutting on

me there's no reason to fire you. What I think we should do is clear the air so that it doesn't happen again."

"Henry, I really am sorry but I had no idea what was going on with you and--"

"I know, I know, and that's why I want to set things straight with you. When you asked about it before I got a little defensive and maybe if I'd been a little more straight with you this whole thing could've been avoided."

"Like you said, it's your business. Obviously there was a lot more going on than I thought."

Henry nodded. "Something like that. When I was young, before I met Monica, I fell in with a bad crowd. I dropped out of college for a while and turned my attention towards the occult. During that time I did a lot of things I wasn't proud of, one of them being summoning that demon. Under its influence I did things that were even worse."

"So you were possessed?"

"Back then I was. It's different when you invite the possession. You're still yourself, in a way, but you can access the demon's powers. No matter how free you think you, are it's still influencing you and moving towards their ultimate goal."

"Do I want to know what that is?" She asked.

He waved a hand. "The usual. The complete corruption of all human life on earth and dominion over their souls, leading to the extinction of all life on this plane of existence."

Lexie shrugged. "Seems reasonable. So how'd you get out from under this thing's thumb?

"When Owen was still a cop he and his old partner Hector were fighting the occult on the side. The two of them found me and helped me regain control of myself. The catch was that because of the spell I'd used to summon the demon it was bound to my soul. As long as I live it's stuck on this plane of existence. I can't have it out there hurting other people so I found a way to trap it within me. When I die, hopefully after a long and full life, it'll go back to whatever Hell it came from."

"Unless some asshole comes along and fucks up the spell, right?"

He smiled. "Something like that." He held out his wrists, which still had the two medallions wrapped around them. "These will work until I get my tattoo fixed."

"Okay," Lexie nodded. "So you're good?"

"Aside from the fact that my family is freaked out and my kids now know a lot more about my business than I ever wanted them to then yes, things are good."

"They really had no idea?"

"No, so it's been an interesting couple of days and they still have a lot of questions. We at least managed to convince them that we're not Satanists, so that's a plus."

"It's something." She sighed. "I am sorry. I just knew that there was something going on and a lot of the time you leave me guessing. But I shouldn't have gone to Don about it."

"I know why you did and I'm going to make sure that something like that doesn't happen again. But yeah, if you have worries in the future bring them to me first, okay?"

"I will. What's going on with Don?"

"Arrested. We're pressing charges and he's insisting that I was possessed and he was just trying to exorcise me."

"So they think he's crazy?"

"Yup. After what he went through he's definitely not making a whole lot of sense, so that helps. Not to mention I still have a few friends in the local precinct that were able to leave out some of the more peculiar aspects of what happened."

Lexie nodded. "Good. Hopefully they put him in a deep hole somewhere. But let this serve as a lesson that you can't fool me when you say everything is fine when it's not. I'll figure it out. Then I may or may not do something dumb."

He chuckled. "Agreed. In that spirit, when Martin gets back we can talk about a little discovery he made."

"That sounds ominous."

"Nope. It's a lead. One that may help us find our troublesome occult object peddler."

She smiled. "Now that's what I like to hear."

****

Don could still see the burning masses of people when he closed his eye. He'd told them everything about Henry, the demon, his magic, and his tattoo but they didn't believe him. They locked him up and gave him things to make him sleep but even through the medicated haze he could still see them, an afterimage burned into his remaining good eye. The worst was that even though his other eye was gone he could still feel something there, burning and gnawing away at his skull trying to get out. Eventually they had to give him stronger drugs and tie him down so that he wouldn't tear at the bandages on his face. While the drugs kept him quiet and the restraints kept his hands off his his bandages neither kept the images of all those people burning out of his mind. He spent his days sitting in a chair looking out a window, looking at the leaves turning on the trees and trying not to think about them rotting and dying.

"Mr. Porter?" one of the orderlies said to him. He hadn't even noticed the man approaching him. He turned his head as much as the sedatives would allow.

"There you are," the orderly said to someone on Don's blind side. "He's pretty doped up so I'm not sure what kind of response you'll be able to get from him."

"No worries," the man's voice said. He came around into Don's line of sight and sat in the chair in front of him. He looked young, with just a hint of age around the eyes, and his blonde hair was stylishly cut short. He had a visitor's pass clipped to the lapel of his tailored black suit. He leaned in, waving a hand in front of Don's face.

"Hey there, buddy," he said with a slight southern

twang. "You in there?"

Don turned his head away, not wanting to have another talk with another lawyer or other pawn in what seemed to be Henry's unending grasp on the legal system. As he did a hand rested on his shoulder, so light he almost didn't feel it. After a second his head became clearer and he realized he wasn't just seeing the man with his own eye but from a couple of feet above his shoulder through someone else's.

"Yeah, he's in there. They've got him on some pretty strong stuff and...oh yeah, there's definitely been a possession. And whatever it was is no joke. Major juice." The voice from above his shoulder was feminine and Don tried to shrink away from her touch to keep her out of his mind.

"He doesn't want to talk to us."

The blonde man in front of him smiled. "S'alright," he leaned down, trying to catch Don's eye again. "We just want to know what happened and who did this to you. That's who we really want."

Don turned back to him. Even with the woman's touch making it a little easier to think and move it still took all his energy to force the word out of his mouth.

"Churchill."

A Bodyguard of Lies

December

"I suppose you're wondering why I called you here," Martin said, leaning back on the couch as Lexie walked into the office.

"No," Lexie scowled, "And I'm not sure I care." She walked past him and took off her jacket. "I spent all morning in court and now I'm going to eat my lunch." She gestured at the pair of hot dogs gripped precariously between her fingers.

Henry was sitting in one of the chairs facing the couch and turned to waved for her to take a seat in the chair next to him. "It's important, I promise." She groaned around a mouthful of semi-edible street food and grudgingly came to sit next to him.

"How'd it go?" Henry asked.

"Eh," Harmony said, wiggling her hand back and forth. "Their lawyer was a dick but I think I answered all the questions they needed. I've got to say, testifying in a divorce trial isn't exactly as fun as I'd thought it would be."

"True," Henry said. "But it helps pay the bills."

Martin gave a deep sigh and turned his laptop around so they could see the screen. "Anyway," he said. "For the real reason we're assembled here."

"Being able to pay the bills means being able to pay your salary, " Henry reminded him.

Martin nodded. "That's an important topic for another time but this is about the research I've been doing on the books that had been given out by our mysterious magic dealer. They part of a set and I think I've finally figured out what it is."

"About time," Lexie said, finishing off the last of her hot dog. "So what do we have?"

"Well, it took some doing but I was able to scan in the covers of the books and check them against photographs of various occult collections and libraries. Needless to say there aren't a lot of those that have pictures proudly displayed on-line so I had to do so--"

"You used a Spooky Google, I get it," she said, twirling impatiently. "What did you find?"

Martin sighed and clicked the trackpad of the laptop and a picture of an etching of a long set of books appeared on the screen. "This is the collected work of Francesco De La

Paizo. He was an exorcist arcane scholar who made extensive notes about his study of demonology and witchcraft during the Spanish Inquisition. Kind of an upside to one of the shittier parts of history."

Lexie pointed at screen. "Did you make a Powerpoint for this?"

"No," Martin said, clicking the trackpad again. An old drawing of a man in Inquisitor's robes came on the screen, with 'Francesco De La Paizo' and some vital statistics typed out underneath him. "Maybe," Martin said clicking ahead to the next slide, a list of titles in two columns.

"So what do we know about these books?" Henry said.

"Well, clearly Frankie was one of your type-A torturing nutjobs. He's got a volume for everything, from demon catalogs to summoning circles to books on divination to the assembling of golems and other supernatural creatures."

"Like the Chalmer's book on making a homunculus?" Lexie said.

"Bingo," Martin said. "And my book on summoning demons. Nineteen volumes all total. Some big, some small."

"That's a lot of books," Henry said, rubbing the thin fuzz of hair on his scalp. "And any one of them could cause serious problems, either deliberately or accidentally."

"Yeah, all we need is some disgruntled cheerleader wanting revenge on the squad that cut her and boom, she summons a horde of zombies to attack the prom," Martin said.

Lexie cocked an eyebrow. "That seems a little too specific."

" After what happened to me I find myself up late at night thinking about how much worse things could have been. Plus I have a very active fantasy life."

"And a sadly stereotypical one. I mean, cheerleaders?" Lexie smirked.

"Anyway," Henry interjected. "The real problem is that we don't know where the rest of these are."

"Actually," Martin grinned. "I've been doing some more digging in the past couple of weeks and I think I've found some good news."

Henry raised an eyebrow. "And you didn't tell me?"

"Awww," Lexie said, patting him on the shoulder. "Does it bother you when a co-worker doesn't share important information with you? Gosh, I wish I could sympathize."

"Alright, alright," Henry said, pushing her hand away. "Point taken. What'd you find out?"

"There aren't that many known collectors of supernatural antiquities and needless to say, these guys aren't trading shit on eBay. When I discovered this Henry tried reaching out to some of the guys that he knew but no one knew anything."

Henry nodded. "The Paizo collection is a pretty hot commodity. I didn't even let on that we had two of the volumes here at the office as people were more interested in finding out what I knew rather than telling me what they did. How did you find out anything?"

"Some of the guys I went to college with have gotten a little more into the deep web than I ever did, and I--"

"Whoa," Lexie interrupted. "The deep web?"

"It's the parts of the internet google doesn't take you to. Off the radar, generally anonymous and usually fully of illegal and nasty shit. Or as you put it 'Spooky Google.'"

"Wonderful. A haven for evil nerds, not with magic."

"Well my evil nerds have been helping me find the areas of the deep web people seem to be talking about trading supernatural paraphernalia. Using that, I was able to do some discreet poking around about the Paizo collection which led me to this." Martin clicked to the next slide, a photo of an Asian man in his sixties. "This is Bernard Park, an art dealer who lives in Mendham. Lots of money, big house, and while he's not one of the biggest collectors of supernatural crap in the country, or even the East Coast, the going theory is that he's the current owner of the collection."

Henry grunted, eyes narrowing.

"You know him?" Lexie asked.

Henry nodded. "I've heard of him. I think Owen met him once or twice."

"Yeah," Martin said, clicking ahead to the next slide. "Then that makes this next part a little easier." On the screen were a series of invoice numbers, dates, and dollar amounts.

The dates stretched back almost ten years, with one payment a year since then. All of the invoices were made out to "Golden Dawn Importers" and started at close to ten thousand dollars and climbed steadily to close to twenty thousand dollars until they ended a couple of months before Owen had died.

"Oh don't tell me," Lexie said.

"Yup," Martin nodded. "Golden Dawn Importers is one of the companies owned by Bernie Park."

"Owen met him once or twice, huh?" Lexie said. Henry let out a long sigh, drumming his fingers on the arm of his chair.

"So you didn't know anything about this?" Martin said.

"I knew that Owen occasionally did some outside jobs but that's it. I figured they were mundane jobs and not stuff like this. Or for that much money."

"Yeah, that brings me back to the paying of the bills part. I've been digging through some of the old financials and things are kind of a giant mess. What I did find out is that these jobs that Owen was doing on the side were some of the highest paying gigs this place had. I've been doing what I can with what's coming in but we're beginning to dip down into the contingency fund without them."

"Oh, fantastic," Lexie said, getting to her feet. "On top of everything else we're broke."

Henry's drumming stopped with a pointed, solid tap.

"Not broke. Broke-ish," Martin said, closing the

laptop. "I mean, there's still money coming in but we may have to start raising rates a little. Maybe start cutting some expenses."

"It won't come to that," Henry said.

"We hope," Lexie said. "This is good work, Martin. I'm sorry, I'm just frustrated."

Martin stopped halfway to his desk and looked back up at her. "Was that a compliment? And an apology? Don't mind me I'm going to wait here for the other shoe to drop. Or in this case, banana."

She shook her head with a little smile as Henry got out of his chair and walked over to his desk. "I mean it. You keep an eye on this deep web stuff. Maybe we can find out more about our friend Bernie. Or even some more paying work."

Martin smiled as he headed back to his desk in the outer office. "Will do."

Lexie turned and Henry was putting on his coat and hat. He was still moving slowly, body not entirely healed from all the cuts and stabs from a couple of weeks ago, but the grimace on his face was from more than just pain from exertion.

"So what's the plan?" She asked.

"The plan," he said, through a mouth of clenched teeth. "Is to drive out to Mendham and see what our friend Mr. Park has to say for himself. Martin!" he yelled out to the outer office. Martin poked his head back in. "Text us Mr. Park's address. We're going to pay him a visit."

Martin looked over at Lexie, who nodded as she headed towards the supply closet. "You got it," he said, heading back to his desk. Her phone vibrated from the text as she strapped on her holster. "Do you need anything from in here?" she said, walking to her desk for her Walther.

Henry shook his head. "I'm hoping you don't need that."

"Better to not need and have than to need and not have, y'know?"

Henry nodded. "Fair enough. Let's go."

The ride was quiet. There wasn't a lot of traffic and they sat in silence until they cleared the tunnel and were in Jersey. Henry drove and Lexie studied the information about Park that Martin was emailing her as he found it.

"He's doing pretty well for himself, that's for sure. From everything that Martin's found he's pretty legit. No sign of sketchy magic dealings. Not so much as an unlikely turn around on an investment or rebound in the stock market."

Henry made a noncommittal noise, eyes focused on the road.

"This doesn't really add up, though," she continued. "Collectors don't just give away things like this, especially if they're one of a kind."

"Yup."

"Plus there's the girl that approached Martin in the bar

and where she fits into all this."

"Uh-huh."

Lexie paused. "Are we going to have a problem?"

He looked over at her. "What do you mean?"

"I mean you look like you're ready to kick this guy's ass - not ask him for information about his books. We go in there guns blazing and he's going to slam the door in our face, so I hope that your mopey road trip face means that you're coming up with a plan."

Henry sighed. "You're right, I just...I wish I knew what he and Owen had going on and why he never told me about it." He looked over at Lexie. "You can say it."

"What?" she said.

"The I told you so. Or the serves me right. Or just pointing out the irony that Owen was keeping secrets like this from me."

She raised her hands. "Hey, it seems pretty obvious already. Plus I figure you've been tortured enough. No pun intended."

He chuckled. "I told Owen everything," he said, shaking his head. "He knew all the dirty shit that I did when I was young, knew all about my past and I figured that he'd told me everything too. The more I think about those last months before he took off and how he acted at the end I realize I didn't know anything. He was playing me. He fucking played me."

"I get it,I really do. But at least we've got a lead now,

right?"

He nodded. "Yeah. And I get why this was so frustrating for you before. Keeping secrets is no way to make a partnership work. I know I've said it before but I'm sorry."

She reached out and put a hand on his. "I'm sorry too. And I know I said it too but I wouldn't want you to feel sensitive all by yourself."

"Thanks," he smirked.

"Hey," she said, "What are partners for?"

"So this is how the other half lives, huh?" Lexie let out a low whistle.

"More like the other 1%." Henry said. As soon as they made it into Morris County the lawns got longer and the houses got bigger and they could tell that whatever Bernard Park had been paying Owen was just pocket change. Bernard Park's house had a big, iron gate in front of its long, winding driveway that led up a hill to a house that just barely peeked out behind trees and impressive landscaping. Henry reached out and buzzed the intercom box next to the gate and a light came on under the security camera.

"Can I help you?" a woman's voice answered over the intercom.

"Yes," he said. "My name is Henry Churchill. I'm here to talk to Mr. Park."

"And what is this regarding?"

"Owen McCabe."

"I'm sorry sir, we don't know any--"

"Tell him its about Owen McCabe and the Paizo collection. He'll know what I'm talking about."

"One moment please," the voice said and the light under the camera clicked off.

"This oughta be good," Lexie said. "What?" She asked, noticing Henry's eyes studying the iron gate and the patterns the bars made.

He pointed at the almost random loops and swirls. "Wards. Designed to keep spirits out. And in. Probably made from cold forged iron, too."

As she stared the gate opened and the intercom clicked on again. "Please drive around to the back. Mr. Park will meet you at the office entrance."

"Oooh, fancy," Lexie said. "I can't wait to rattle this guy's cage and see what shakes out." They drove the Gremlin up the steep driveway and the house revealed itself. It was modern and brick, two stories with several peaks and gables and a tower in the rear corner. The driveway led them through an arched covered carport and on the other side a young woman in a prim business suit and tightly wound hair waved them to a small parking area in front of a three car garage in the back of the house.

"Oh we have got to move out to the suburbs," Lexie said as they got out.

"Not a chance," Henry muttered as the young woman approached the car.

"I'm Ms. Saunders," she said with a nod. "Follow me please, Mr. Park is waiting in his office." She led them inside and into a spacious room with floor to ceiling bookshelves, a set of leather chairs and couches, and a desk in the center. From the far end of the room a pair of heavy wooden doors opened and Bernard Park walked through.

"You must be Mr. Churchill," he said. He looked much like he did in the picture Martin had found, but with grayer, slicked back hair and wearing a light sweater and khakis that made him look like he just stepped out of a fashion magazine.

"I am. It's nice to meet you, Mr. Park." Henry extended a hand and he shook it, taking notice of the antique silver bracelets and rings on his hand. "This is my partner, Lexie Winston."

"Charmed," she said, offering a hand. He took it and shook, the corner of his mouth twitching in a smile.

"Ah," Bernard said. "She must be Mr. McCabe's replacement."

"So you knew I worked with Owen?" Henry said.

Park nodded with a wry smile. "Oh yes. He and I had a very long history together. He mentioned you with great fondness. Please, come into my office. Would either of you care for some coffee?"

"Sure," Lexie said. "Black is fine." Henry declined and Ms. Saunders retreated from the reception area as Park led them into his office.

It was at least twice as large as the outer room and with the same floor to ceiling shelves. On the far wall there were several tall windows looking out at a back yard that stretched as far as the eye could see. Throughout the room in neatly spaced rows there were stone pedestals, all about a foot square and with a glass case on top. In each case there was a different item: a vase, a box, a stone, and other curiosities. Henry could feel magical energy radiating around them

Park took a seat behind his expansive desk and waved them to do likewise on the large, overstuffed leather chairs in front of it. Lexie sat, putting her feet up on the edge of his desk. Henry smiled and took a slow circuit around the office, stopping to admire the items in the cases.

Park cleared his throat and Henry turned around to see him glaring at Lexie over the tip of her boot. "Do you mind?"

"Do you?" She replied, raising an eyebrow at him. She leaned back, her fingers laced behind her head and letting her jacket fall open to show the butt of her pistol.

"I do," he said, and she shrugged, putting her feet on the floor with a wide, fake smile.

"You have some exceptionally rare pieces here," Henry said. "Is that a Mayan Death Stone?" He gestured towards the case and felt a wave of magical energy push his hand back.

Park turned to look at Henry, expression softening slightly. "If not it's a fantastic forgery. But please, sit. I should say that despite what you may have heard the Paizos are no longer in my possession."

"But they were, huh?" Lexie said, sitting up and slapping the edge of his desk and bringing Park's attention back to her. She looked over at Henry with a smile "You owe me twenty bucks."

Park grimaced. "Either way, I no longer have them. And since Mr. McCabe had passed away I'm curious as to what the purpose of your visit is."

"To be honest," Henry said, stopping in his circuit around the room. "I'm just a bit curious as to what your relationship with my former partner was." He came to an empty spot in the room and looked down at the carpet and saw there was a faint indentation the size of the other display cases. Henry reached his hand out and passed it through the space above it.

"Well, not to be too blunt but I believe that was between Mr. McCabe and myself."

"Yeah, but he's dead so what's the harm, right?" Lexie said.

"Be that as it may," Park said, crinkling his face in disdain. "My business with Mr. McCabe was private. If he chose not to share that with his associates then I'm afraid that's not my problem."

"So who did you get after he died?" Henry said, walking back to the front of the desk.

"Excuse me?" Park looked up at him, trying to mask his surprise with feigned confusion.

"Who did you get to do your wards this time around? As much as it bugs me that Owen was doing casting work on the side, especially since that's my forte, I'm interested in who you got to strengthen the wards on your cases this time around since Owen wasn't available. Did she contact you or did you find her? And did she take the Paizo manuscripts in payment or did something else happen to them?"

Park's mouth opened and then closed, the color draining from his face.

"Coffee?" Miss Sanders said, holding a silver tray with three cups of coffee.

"Lady, you may need to get me some popcorn to go with it," Lexie said, taking a cup from the tray.

Henry turned back to Park, who was regaining his composure. "I don't know what you're talking about."

Henry reached across the desk and put a hand over Park's. Park tried to pull his hand away but Henry held firm. Henry stared into his face and began the words of a spell. There was a sudden push of resistance and the color began to drain from Park's face.

"Now, you don't need to lie to me because I can feel the magic coming off of those cases and I can tell you don't have the juice to pull off casting them yourself. But you're smart enough to have some personal wards and charms in place." Henry tapped his thumb on the cluster of antique silver bracelets on his wrist. "These probably. And perhaps some others since you don't strike me as the tattoo sort."

Park pulled away again but Henry held tight. "I don't give a fuck about you or your collection. I'm curious about your relationship with Owen but that's not the reason we're here. What I really want is the woman who has the collection now. She's hurt people and I want to put a stop to it. Tell me what I want to know and we can go our separate ways."

"My sympathies," Park said. Henry released his grip and Park flexed his hand with an annoyed grimace. "But I don't share business information with strangers. Ms. Saunders?"

He felt her hand on his arm without hearing her move at all. Henry turned his head to see Ms. Saunders balancing the tray with one hand and her other clamped onto his shoulder. Behind her, Lexie had gotten to her feet, hand reaching into her jacket. Henry shook his head slightly and Lexie withdrew it with a scowl, still keeping her position behind Ms. Saunders.

"Now," Park smiled. "If there's nothing else perhaps we can end this impromptu visit. I do have other work to attend to."

Henry nodded, releasing his grip on Park's hand and standing up straight. Ms. Saunders let go of Henry's shoulder as well. "Fine," he said. "But you should know that whoever this person was she's an amateur. Worse, she's been giving away the manuscripts. If you help us find her then I can probably get them back to you. Something to think about, especially since you know how dangerous things like that can be in untrained, amateurish hands. Not to mention the kind of unwanted attention it can attract."

Park's smile wavered he motioned towards the door.

Lexie finished her coffee in one quick gulp and slapped the empty cup face down on Park's desk. "Great coffee," she said, smiling at Ms. Saunders impassive glare.

As they walked out Henry reached towards one of the glass cases. He closed his eyes and whispered the words to a spell. There was a flash of light and an audible crack of energy. Henry looked over his shoulder at Park, whose face was furrowed with a deep scowl.

"See?" Henry said. "Amateur."

"That was impressive," she said as they walked to the car.

"That," he said, putting as much concentration into waking steadily as he could, "was harder than it looked."

"You okay?"

He nodded. "I will be. But I think I need you to drive."

***

In the week that followed Henry, Lexie, and Martin

poured through everything they could find on Bernard Park, trying and failing to find anything in his life or business they could use as leverage against him. His mundane business dealings, mostly in importing and exporting art and antiques, were impeccable and all of his associates and employees were above reproach. He paid his taxes, he gave to charities, and was even active in his local church.

There were mentions of him and speculations about his collection on the deep web but nothing concrete. Henry looked over the list of items it was rumored he had that Martin compiled and Henry marked off the ones that he'd seen in their brief visit.

"There's actually something called a Death Stone?" Martin asked.

"Yeah," Henry said. "And it's as bad as it sounds."

"This can't be right," Lexie said, tracing a finger along the screen of her laptop.

"What?"

"I was checking the local news in Mendham, trying to see if there's been any fallout from Park having all that magical crap stockpiled. Everything was fine until this past year."

"What's changed?" He said, walking over to her.

She pointed at the screen. "According to this, their crime rate has gone up twelve hundred percent in the past year."

"That's gotta be a typo," Martin said, joining them.

Henry shook his head. "I don't think so. There'd only

been a handful of murders in all of Morris County in the past couple of years. In the past year there have been six in Mendham alone. Felony assaults are up, too." When they looked deeper they found that starting last January there were dozens of instances in the town's police blotter of violent offenses that occurred suddenly and with no doubt as to the perpetrator. A mother was arrested for beating her thirteen year old daughter so badly she ended up in a coma for a week. A man shot his wife after discovering she'd had an affair and then went to her office and shot six other people while trying to kill the man she'd been sleeping with. A 68 year old woman poisoned her son, daughter-in-law and two grandchildren with cake she'd brought to a birthday party. As the year had gone on it had been the one of the most violent and tumultuous in suburban New Jersey history, culminating in an incident last week at Mendham High School where a fight had broken out at a football game and cops dispersed the crowd with tear gas, rubber bullets, and batons. Almost two dozen people were sent to the hospital, nearly half of them in critical condition.

"I don't think there's been a crime spree in the suburbs since they thought there was a serial killer in my home town a couple of years ago," Martin said.

Henry walked over the list Martin had been compiling of items it was suspected that Park had collected. "I don't think it's a coincidence," he said, bringing the list over to the others and tapping his finger on one of the items. "Not if he actually had one of these."

"But why just now?" Martin said.

"There was an empty spot in his office where something used to be, and whatever it was had been enchanted with the same kind of magic that had been used to bind the other artifacts in the gallery."

"So something happened to it," Lexie said. "Something probably caused by our little amateur."

Henry nodded, walking back to his desk. "Exactly," he said. "And that means we've got something." He picked up the phone and dialed Park's number.

"Mr. Churchill?" Ms. Saunders answered. "I thought Mr. Park made it clear that he wasn't interested in discussing his affairs with you."

"He did," Henry nodded. "But you can tell him that not only might I be able to retrieve the Paizo manuscripts I can also re-enchant the wards on his collection, correctly this time. I can also replace his Fury Vase."

There was silence at the end of the line and then finally she said "I'll let him know." There was a click and the line went quiet.

"Well?" Lexie said.

"I think I'm on hold," Henry said, putting the call on speaker.

"Mr. Churchill," Park said, coming back on the line a few moments later. "I thought I'd made myself clear."

"You did," Henry said. "But that was after we did some digging and realized how much of a screw up the person you'd hired to replace Owen was. I figured you'd want an opportunity to get someone competent to help you out, as well as replace all of the things she cost you."

"I'm not entirely sure I...am I on speaker?"

"Hey Bernie!" Lexie called from her desk. "Lexie Winston here. Man, I've never seen someone so adamant not to let someone clean up their mess for them."

Park sighed into the phone. "Is there anyone else there? I prefer not to discuss my business so publicly."

"Just our receptionist," Lexie added.

"I'm more than a receptionist," Martin balked. "I mean, I do the books too and--"

"So you're like a secretary. That sits where a receptionist sits," she said.

"I'm an assistant," Martin said. "I'm literally assisting you right now!"

Henry finally caught their attention with a frantic wave.

"Are they done?" Park said.

"I wish," grumbled Henry, "but you still need our help. All I want in return is a name and how you got in contact with her."

"What makes you feel like I need your help?"

"Because she broke your Fury Vase," Henry said. "I

don't know if it was during the initial casting or if the vase degraded over time, although the latter seems a bit more likely seeing as how she's got your books."

"And what makes you think I hav...had a Fury Vase?"

"I don't know," Lexie said. "Do people in Mendham usually go on killing sprees at the drop of the hat, or is that a new thing that they started since you had our mutual friend over?"

"I don't know anything about that."

"Bullshit," she said.

"Mr. Park," Henry said, "You're wasting time. The Vase broke, the Furies got out and they're in Mendham. You can't be so blind as to not notice the change in the atmosphere. People are killing each other. Specifically, parents trying to kill children, people violently avenging betrayal and now, most recently, an extremely violent reaction to the disrespect of youth and authority. All things that the classical Greek Furies are invoked to punish. It's only a matter of time before the town tears itself apart and all the magical wards on Earth aren't going to keep a mob of enraged people from your door when that town tears itself apart. Not to mention the kind of attention something like that would bring, especially from those looking for evidence of the supernatural."

The line was quiet. "And you think you can fix this?"

"I know that I'm going to do what I can to get those Furies contained regardless of what we decide here. Now I'm willing to bet that you'd be interested to have them back in your collection so you can do...well, whatever it is guys like you do with things like this. You tell me what I want to know and you'll get them back. As well as the Paizo volumes I have."

"And you'd re-enchant the wards on my collection?"

Lexie grinned, miming using a fishing pole to reel in a catch.

"Yes," Henry said, feeling less satisfied.

"Very well," he said. "When?"

"It'll take me a little bit of time to gather what I need for the ritual but I can do it by the end of the week. Do you have the remains of the old vase?"

"I do."

"If you allow me to take a look at them I can--"

"I'm going to be leaving for Saltsburg in a couple of hours," Park interrupted. "I won't be back until Thursday afternoon. Not to mention the fact I'm not willing to hand anything over until I have what I want.

"Of course you're not." Lexie rolled her eyes.

"You're the ones that want information," Park said. "I still have time to find someone else to take care of my collection."

"It's fine," Henry said.

"I thought as much," Park said, reveling in his little victory. "I'll put Ms. Saunders on the line to arrange it."

***

"Hey Henry," Martin said the next day. "You should take a look at this."

He set the laptop down on the edge of Henry's desk and pointed at the article on the screen. "We've been looking for all kinds of stuff about Bernie and his holdings and I realized there was something we had overlooked. Check this out," Henry read the article but stopped when he got to one of the pictures halfway down the page.

"How about that," he said as Martin nodded at his shoulder.

"Yeah I thought that could be something."

"Not just something," Henry said. "I think it's going to come in handy as well. We need to find out everything we can about this." The two kept digging for a couple of hours until Lexie came back from her surveillance of Mendham.

"Find anything interesting?" Henry asked her.

"Well, things seemed mostly normal," she said, hanging up her coat. "Stores were open, holiday shoppers out in force. People were sort of friendly but there's definitely something that feels...off about the place. But this is the real kicker." She took a piece of colored paper out of the pocket and held it up for them to read.

THURSDAY NIGHT! 8PM!

MENDHAM COMMUNITY CENTER!
TOWN HALL MEETING TO DISCUSS THE
INCIDENT
AT THE MENDHAM HIGH FOOTBALL GAME!
TOWN OFFICIALS AND PTA MEMBERS WILL BE IN
ATTENDANCE!

Someone had crossed out the word "incident" and scrawled "bullshit" in black sharpie next to it.

"Wow, that's…" Martin started but was interrupted by Henry's sharp, angry sigh. "Wait, this Thursday?"

"Yup," Lexie said. "You had said that we'd need to find a way to track the Furies down and get relatively close before we could trap them again. Given how heated it looks like things are going to be I'd say it's the safest of bets that they'll be there."

"So we have to move this up a day," Martin said. "Didn't the Rabbi say he'd have this ready on Thursday anyway?"

"Thursday evening," Henry said, tenting his fingers in front of his face. "There's a certain amount of charge the charms for the ritual will need. I can check with Abraham to see how close we can cut it but I don't want to half-ass this and find ourselves in the same spot a few months from now."

After a flurry of phone calls they convinced Park (through Ms. Saunders) to meet them Thursday evening shortly after his return. Abraham, thankfully, was a bit more responsive and said that he'd be comfortable letting them have the charms in the afternoon but any earlier would have grave consequences.

"That's a pretty small window," Lexie said.

"There's no chance we can get the wards done before the meeting starts?" Martin asked.

"Based on what Park told me he needs we're looking at at least a couple of hours. Maybe more, depending on how much he actually has that he wants me to ward. He wouldn't even give me an estimate on how many pieces he had."

"Douche," Martin mumbled.

"We're going to need more people," Lexie said after a few moments.

Henry raised an eyebrow at her. "We're a little understaffed."

"Yeah, but it seems like we're going to have to find a way to do the wards and capture the Furies at the same time, unless we want to let them turn a town hall meeting into a bloodbath--"

"Which we don't," Henry said.

"Exactly. So we need someone with us who can do the ceremony to capture the Furies since Park only wants you working on the wards."

Henry rubbed his chin. "Okay, but Park was also clear that he didn't want anyone outside our office involved in this so who do you..." He trailed off, turning to look at Martin.

"Why are...oh no," he said, raising his hands and getting up from the couch. "My flirtation with magic and the forces of darkness was just a one night stand. No thank you, hard pass."

Henry waved his hand. "The ritual isn't dangerous. It just requires someone with magical aptitude."

"Can't Lexie do it? She's got loads of aptitude."

Lexie shook her head. "Not for magic. One of our first cases had me help Henry try to cast a binding spell on a demon and it didn't go well. At all. Apparently I'm too closed minded."

"Really?" Martin said. "You? Perish the thought."

"It's a matter of energies. Hers, and most other people's, flow one way. Others go the opposite. Some more, some less. I'm sure yours are more than enough, especially since you were able to summon that demon." Henry didn't add that most demons wanted to be summoned and they didn't make it that hard so they could ensnare and manipulate those foolish enough to try.

Martin sat back down, running a hand through his hair. "Shit, dude. I just...what if something goes wrong?"

"It's not like you'll be doing it alone," Lexie said, patting him on the shoulder. "Henry will be able to do the wards himself and I'll have your back while you're casting. Plus Henry will be able to run you through it a bunch of times before then." Behind his back Lexie shrugged, giving Henry a quizzical look.

"For real?" he said, looking up at Henry.

"Absolutely," Henry said, trying to keep as straight a face as possible.

The next couple days were a blur of activity as Martin dove into studying for the ceremony and Lexie continued to scout out Mendham and the community center where the town meeting was being held. Henry kept up the mundane work that they had by himself, which meant a couple of later nights. After locking up the office the night before the ceremony he turned to head down the hallway when he heard a pair of footsteps coming up the stairs and then a then a laugh that took him a moment to identify as Lexie's. He'd never heard the kind of unguarded warmth radiating from her before and for a moment he wanted to duck out of the way to give her privacy. He stood his ground and they came around the corner, Lexie with a glowing smile on her face and her arm around the shoulders of the much shorter Harmony, who was leaning into her with a relaxed smile of her own.

"Hey," he said, as the two stopped short in front of him. "I was just heading home."

"Sure," Lexie said. "I just wanted to grab some stuff from the office since I'm...staying at Harm's tonight. Harmony, this is Henry Churchill."

Harmony extended a hand and Henry shook it with a nod, the two trying to give each other sincere smiles. "Harmony

Valley," she said. "Nice to finally meet the elusive partner."

"Thanks. I could say the same." Henry said, the last name giving off a buzz of familiarity, despite the fact he hadn't heard Lexie mention it before.

"Ugh," Lexie said, unlocking the office and stepping inside. "Don't use that word. She's my girlfriend. You're my partner. Very different things."

"I should hope so," Harmony said as Lexie disappeared into the office, leaving the two alone in the hallway.

"Valley," he said. "Why is that name so familiar?"

"Aside from my parents' sense of humor?" Harmony smirked. "You met my Dad, George. Probably around twenty years ago."

Henry nodded, forcing his face to remain neutral. "Yeah, I remember now. He was a good guy."

"Yeah. Took me a while to figure it out after he took off, but he came back about three years ago when my mom died and we made our peace."

"Well that's good. He did leave pretty suddenly."

"That's a bit of an understatement," she said. "He told me the reason he left and it was hard to believe at first, but what he showed me and what I've seen since makes it a lot easier to swallow."

"I can imagine," he said, looking into the office to see if Lexie was in earshot. "How much of this did you tell Lexie?"

"Most of it," she smirked. "The important parts, at

least, including my dad's...gift, as he put it. She and I don't really do secrets," she added with a pointed narrowing of her eyes.

"Even if they may put her in danger? Or make her a target?"

Her smile hardened. "Secrets only put people in danger when they're still secrets. I figure you'd have learned that by now."

Henry opened his mouth to reply when they heard Lexie walking towards them.

"All set" Lexie said, stepping back into the hallway with some papers tucked under her arm. When she realized that they'd stopped talking she froze. "What?"

"Nothing," Harmony said with a smile. "Just shop talk. You ready?"

"Just a sec. I want to talk to him about the thing."

"Right," Harmony said with nod. "I'll just go wait in the car."

Henry watched her leave. "There's a thing?"

"Yeah, while we were in Mendham Harmony and I were talking and...what?" she stopped. "What's that look?"

"Nothing," he said, trying to regain his neutral expression. "But I have a feeling I know what you're going to say."

"And that look tells me you don't really approve."

"It's not that it's just...you're going to need some help

keeping Martin covered during the spell, aren't you?"

She nodded. "Yeah. That community center is big and there's going to be a lot of people there. When they get all riled up by Furies I'm going to need all hands on deck to keep him safe."

Henry nodded. "You're right. It's a good call. I'm assuming she's more than willing?"

"Yup. And she may have said something along the lines that she'd be there to help me no matter what you or I said."

"That sounds about right. Just...be careful, okay?"

Lexie patted him on the shoulder. "Always."

***

"Is it bad that I kind of want this town to tear itself apart just on principle?" Harmony said as they pulled into a parking spot across from the Mendham Community Center.

"Not at all," Martin said from the backseat. "I grew up in a town like this and felt that way for eighteen years."

The three got out of Harmony's Mustang and watched the crowd of people filing in through the community center's doors.

"You ready for this?" Lexie asked Martin.

Martin took a deep breath and nodded. "Yeah. I mean, there's only so much cramming you can do before an exam right? Although this is less pass/fail and more pass/mass panic destroys a town and potentially kills hundreds."

Harmony patted him on the shoulder. "Well as long as you haven't stressed about it you should be fine."

Lexie took the old leather duffle bag out of the backseat. "You're going to do great. Everyone make sure they have their amulets in place."

The three of them waited until the crowd trying to get inside thinned out and then made their way into the community center. The two story building had a glass facade that stretched nearly to the roof. Inside the atrium was filled with various inspirational and historical pieces of artwork by and about "prominent community members" with a wide curving staircase on the far wall that led up to a second floor balcony that looked down on them. Next to the staircase were sets of double doors leading into the auditorium portion of the center where the meeting was to be held and to the left of that was a hallway leading back to the classroom and smaller meeting areas that Lexie and Harmony had scouted out earlier in the week.

The trio made their way through the crowd that was streaming into the auditorium doors under the watchful eye of several police offers that looked like they were more equipped to keep the peace at an Israeli-Palestinian Friendship festival rather than a town hall meeting of disgruntled suburbanites. Lexie led them towards the largest space between officers, hoping that their veering off from the crowd and down the hall would go unnoticed. As the crowd squeezed together to make it through the open doors they already began to jostle and shove more than seemed necessary and Lexie had to reach back to grab Harmony's hand so she didn't lose sight of the smaller woman as she pushed Martin through with her other hand.

As they made it out of the edge of the crowd and started down the hallway one of the cops turned his attention towards them, looking the two women up and down over the gold frames of his mirrored glasses he'd made the bold choice of wearing inside.

"Help you ladies?" he asked as he ambled towards them.

"No, we're good," Harmony said, turning back and flashing him a smile as they kept moving. "We were just going to sign up for the craft fair before the meeting." She motioned down the hall towards the bulletin boards back by the rooms the two had scouted days before.

"You into crafts too, fella?" He nodded at Martin, following them. He was close enough now that Lexie could read the name "Preston" above the badge that was affixed to his bulletproof vest.

"Yeah, I love a good...craft," Martin said, almost coming to a stop before Harmony nudged him along.

"I bet you do." Preston's eyes narrowed as he looked down at Lexie and Harmony's still clasped hands. He sneered, curling his certainly non-ironic thick mustache like a dying caterpillar. "You ladies have fun."

"Classic," Martin muttered as they headed down the hallway.

When they reached the door of the room they'd scouted Lexie checked over her shoulder to make sure Preston's attention was back on the rest of the crowd coming in before jimmying the lock open with the lock release gun Henry had acquired.

"Alright," Lexie said, relocking the door behind her. "Martin, start setting up. Harm, head into the meeting and keep us posted as to what's going on. If something hinky starts happening I want to know about it and get ready."

"Hinky?" she asked with a smirk.

"Yes dear, hinky. Strange, unusual, Fury-like. Or if nothing happens at all and it turns out this whole thing was a big to do for nothing."

"Got it," Harmony said, dropping the duffle bag and getting on her toes to give Lexie a quick kiss.

"Just get to work," Lexie said, feeling herself blush. "Don't kiss me in front of my secretary."

"I'm an assistant," Martin said, not looking up from the diagram in the folio with instructions for laying out the urn and the rest of the components.

"Well you're not assisting now, buddy.," Harmony said, leaving the room with a wink. Lexie relocked the door behind her and checked the contents of the bag again. "Are we all set?" she said, handing him the small bag of shards.

"I think so," he said, running his hands through his hair with a nervous sigh. He looked up at her. "The last time I did this I had a couple of beers in me. Plus I didn't think it was going to work."

"You'll be fine," she said. "You heard what Henry said, you've got aptitude."

"Ma always said I'd figure out what I was special at one day."

With a deep breath, he made a ring of the broken shards around the plain, garden store urn that the Rabbi had prepared as a new vessel for the Furies. "Okay," he said, placing a hand on the lip of the Urn and looking down at the folio opened in front of him. "Here goes...something."

After the others left it took Henry a little over an hour to walk the boundaries of the grounds, swinging several of his medallions and repeating the words of one of the most potent protection and warding spells he knew. By the time he made it back to the house he was damp with sweat and his breath was labored. When he walked into Park's study the man looked up from his laptop and raised an eyebrow at him.

"This level of casting isn't too much for you, is it?" he asked with what Henry had come to realize was his signature blend of arrogance and annoyance.

Henry shook his head, taking a seat in one of the chairs in front of his desk. "I'm fine. It's just been a difficult month. I assure you that the wards will be more than sufficient."

"What kind, if I may ask?"

"Akkadian," Henry said. "Perfected in the 17th century by a Flemmish caster who studied in China. Quite effective."

"DuMont?" Park said, leaning forward with a predatory gleam in his eyes. "I'd heard he'd designed a series of wards but my understanding was that most of his work was lost in the Napoleonic Wars."

"Most," Henry said. "Not all."

"Fascinating. I'd love to hear how you acquired them."

"It's a boring story. And no, they aren't for sale."

Park sighed with thwarted avarice. "Pity. Would you care for a refreshment while you gather your strength?"

"Water would be lovely," Henry said.

"Certainly," Ms. Saunders said from behind him. "Anything else?"

"No," Henry said, turning and giving her a smile and nod. She smiled back and walked back through the door that he hadn't heard open.

"She's quite handy," Henry said, turning back to Park.

"Indeed. Indispensable."

"Real nice house. I couldn't help but admire it as I was making my rounds. An impressive amount of room."

Park gave a thin smile. "I enjoy my space. Plus it gives

me more room to display my treasures."

"I bet. I'm assuming you have the rest of your more dangerous pieces elsewhere on the grounds then?"

Park nodded. "The previous owners put in a wine cellar that I've turned into a vault."

"That must have been quite a renovation," Henry said. This time he heard Ms. Saunders approaching behind him and he turned, taking the glass of water from her with a smile.

"If you don't mind," Henry said. "I'd like to check in with my people before I continue."

"Of course," Park said, getting up. "I'll give you some privacy while I prepare the vault for you."

Henry nodded and after Ms. Saunders and Park left the room he took out his phone and dialed Lexie.

"Please tell me you accidentally burned his house down," Lexie answered.

"No, but the first round of protection wards are up. I'm taking a little break before I do the individual ones. How're things there?"

"Fine," Lexie said, sounding a little unsure. "It seems like the meeting is rowdy but just 'cops beat up teenagers rowdy' not Furies rowdy."

"How's Martin doing?"

Lexie sighed and it sounded like she was walking a little ways. "He's okay. We had a couple of false starts but I think he's figured it out now."

Henry sighed. "Good. If he does have it right then you're probably going to--"

He was interrupted by a series of loud bangs from her end of the line. "You were saying?" she said. "Gotta go. Keep you posted," she said and then the line went dead. Henry stared at his phone for a moment, grimacing.

"Is there a problem, Mr. Churchill?" Ms. Saunders said from behind him.

"No," Henry said, getting to his feet with a grimace.

"That's good. Mr. Park asked for me to bring you down to the arcane vault to continue your work," she said with a smile and a wave of her hand towards the door to the office.

"Of course he did," Henry said. As he walked past her he stopped, staring at her. She looked at him with a smile and eyes that seemed to be staring right through him. "He's a real piece of work, isn't he?"

She focused on him and her smile wavered a little. "Pardon?"

"Your boss. He's a real jerk to be keeping you here so late. I'm sure you'd much rather be at home. With your family."

She blinked rapidly at him, the smile going slack. "No, I'm right where I belong," she finally said, smile popping back into place. "Right this way, please."

"Sure," Henry said, following after her. "Whatever you say."

The door handle had started rattling slightly at first but when whoever was on the other side realized it was locked the rattling became frantic and turned into pounding on the door. Lexie texted Harmony as she rushed over to the door, bracing it with her shoulder. Martin looked up at her with wide eyes as he tried to hold the papers in his hand steady while he recited the spell for the third time. Both previous attempts had ended with fumbled pronunciation and then a stream of panicked, self-deprecating profanity. Lexie nodded at him and waved at him to keep going.

"Who's in there?" Came the yell from the other side. "This area is off limits!"

Lexie unlocked the door and opened it a crack, keeping her body against it and her feet braced. The officer on the other side, head cleanly shaven and whose badge said "Briggs," had one hand raised to pound on the door again and the other resting on his still holstered pistol. "Can I help you?" Lexie asked.

"What are you doing in here?" the officer growled at her. "This area is off limits!"

"I thought this was a community center. We're part of the community."

"The center is only open during certain hours," Briggs growled at her. He was squeezing the grip of the pistol to some rhythm only he could hear.

"Well that's not very welcoming of y--"

"What is he doing?" Briggs said, spotting Martin over her shoulder. "You! Stop!" He yanked his pistol from the holster and slammed into the door with his full and not unimpressive body weight.

She released her hold on the door and stepped aside, sending Briggs staggering into the room. She pulled the tactical baton from her belt and extended it as he gained his balance and raised his pistol towards Martin. She swung the baton into Briggs' ribs and he recoiled in pain, losing his aim at Martin who was still reading the words of the spell in frenzied rush, eyes going from paper to cop as if he was trying to decide which was a bigger threat.

Briggs turned towards Lexie, face scarlet and veins on his head throbbing wildly, but thankfully forgetting Martin. She swung the baton at him again and he blocked it with his forearm, the impact giving off a crunch that she could both hear and feel. Briggs could clearly do neither, raising his pistol towards her. She stepped out of the line of fire and swung the baton into the hand holding the gun, making him pull it back as he tried to get her in his sights. She stepped within his arms reach and swung the baton up into his elbow. She could feel the crunch in his arm again but the impact made him discharge his pistol into the air. She stepped behind him and hit him behind his ear, dropping him to the ground.

She glanced over at Martin. The gunshot hadn't broken his concentration as she had feared but instead his attention was locked onto the Urn in front of him, his voice rising steadily as he kept repeating the words of the spell with no stammers or pauses this time. His eyes were wider and more bloodshot and his hands stretched outward, fingers curled and trembling as if he was clawing the air above the urn apart.

There was a rustle of movement behind her and as she turned a hand grabbed at her hair, missed, and then gripped her jacket at the shoulder. She pulled away but Briggs, a stream of red pouring from the back of his head and down his neck, held firm. Lexie swung the baton but he caught her wrist, snarling with rage.

"Stop. Resisting," he growled.

Lexie twisted, trying to escape his grasp but we was locked on to her. He opened his mouth to say something else when Harmony leaped onto his back, locking her legs around his waist and her arm under his chin. He staggered backwards, off balance, giving Lexie an opportunity to pull her wrist out of his hand. As Harmony hooked her other arm around the back of his head and pushed it forward, completing the sleeper hold, Lexie swung the baton into Briggs' solar plexus. He coughed out the remaining air in his lungs and let go of Lexie's shoulder, grabbing feebly at Harmony's arms around his neck. Lexie reared back, took aim, and cracked the baton against his temple, dropping him to the ground.

"You okay?" Harmony said, climbing off of him. "I came as soon as I heard the gunshot."

"Great," Lexie said. "I was hoping this place was better insulated."

"No such luck. People were already freaking out in there but it didn't seem like they knew what that was. Hopefully--" Harmony was cut off by a crash and a sudden chorus of yells.

"Shit," Lexie said, running for the door with Harmony close behind. They opened the door a crack so they could see down the hallway and into the atrium at the front of the building and the chaos that had spilled into there.

"I think this counts as hinky," Harmony said. The concerned citizens of Mendham were now taking their concerns out on the small group of police officers that were trying to corral them back into the auditorium. Half of the citizens looked to be trying to run for the exits while the others were screaming at the cops to do something about the gunshot they'd heard. The police, on the other hand, were trying to keep everyone inside "for their protection," something they kept yelling over and over again as they waved batons at the panicked crowd. One of the men closest to the front doors, a well-dressed middle aged Hispanic man, dashed forward when the cop nearest to him was turned away. He made it only a few feet when the cop spun and swung his baton into the man's head, dropping him to the ground in a spray of blood. The crowd of people surged forward and the cops stood their ground, swinging their batons wildly and dropping screaming, well-dressed citizenry left and right.

"I really hope this is working," Lexie said. "Because if it's not we're royally fucked."

Harmony looked over her shoulder at Martin. "Babe, I think we might be fucked either way."

Lexie turned and saw that a ring of twisting black smoke had appeared above Martin, pulsing with ribbons of crimson light. Martin's concentration was fixed solely on the vase in front of him, his face so drained of color it was nearly translucent. His chanting of the spell continued, his voice more powerful than his drained features let on. She took a couple of steps towards him and could feel something pushing back against her, as if she was suddenly walking up a steep hill.

There was a crash behind her and Lexie rushed back to the door. Across the hallway and only a few feet up from them Preston and a younger woman had tumbled through one of the emergency exits of the auditorium and into the hallway, locked in a frantic struggle. They spun towards them, one of the woman's hands grabbing the lapel of Preston's uniform and the other slapping and clawing at his face. Preston's hand was fumbling at his belt, trying to get his baton out while fending her off with his free hand.

Harmony took a step forward but Lexie grabbed her arm. As she pulled Harmony back towards their room the woman managed to catch Preston's forehead with her nails, scratching down his face and knocking his glasses askew. With blood trickling down into his maddeningly wide eye he roared and pushed forward, slamming the woman into the wall and stunning her as he pulled out his baton.

"You! Are! Under! Arrest!" he screamed punctuating each word with a blow to her chest.

The savage display stopped Lexie in her tracks, suddenly torn between secrecy and the fury crackling in her brain. In the time it took her to realize they needed to get back inside the conference room Preston noticed them. He raised his baton to point at them, his head turning slowly so he could stare with his exposed and bloodied eye.

"You," he growled. "are under arrest."

"Like hell," Lexie said, backing up and pulling Harmony along with her. Preston charged after them and Lexie slammed the door shut just as he plowed into it. The impact pushed the door open a few inches and Lexie felt her feet skidding along the no-longer fashionable carpet until Harmony leaned into it as well.

"We need to barricade the door," Lexie yelled over the rising volume of Martin's incantation of the spell.

"We need to get the fuck out of here," Harmony said.

Lexie grabbed the nearest table and dragged it to the door, wedging it under the door handle. She turned and pointed at the swirls of crackling smoke above Martin's head. "We have to wait until he's--" Martin's chanting abruptly stopped, making her last few words uncomfortably loud.

"That could be a good sign," Harmony said.

Arcs of red lighting shot down in a ring around Martin. Before she could tell her to get to cover there was a burst of red light and Lexie was blown back by a wave of force. When she picked herself up off the floor she saw the black clouds were coalescing into three shapes above the scorch marks the lightning had left on the carpet. Martin had been knocked backwards and was sprawled out on the ground, eyes closes and not moving. The urn had toppled over and wobbled dangerously close to the edge of the table. Harmony had been thrown in the other direction and was lying next to a toppled over table. Lexie crawled towards her, keeping an eye on the swirling columns of smoke behind her.

"Harm," Lexie said, rolling her over.

"Wha?" Harmony mumbled. There was a knot growing on her forehead where she must've collided with the table.

"Get up," Lexie said, trying to pull her to standing. "We've got trouble."

"No shit," Harmony said looking over Lexie's shoulder.

Lexie turned and saw that the three clouds of smoke had solidified into three female bodies with skin so deep and cosmically black that glancing at it began to give her vertigo. They wore loose robes that were just as black but shimmering with ribbons of deep scarlet, and on each of their backs were dark scarlet wings, dotted with black that pulsed like a field of dead stars. Their heads were snarling and canine with glowing crimson eyes, jet black teeth, and twisted antlers jutting out of their foreheads. They swayed in unison, teeth bared and nostrils flaring, standing so tall the tips of their horns just barely touched the ceiling.

"I guess it worked," Lexie said, and the Furies all turned to look at them.

"What's this?" Henry asked, walking over to one of the empty display stands in the back of the converted wine cellar.

"An unused display," Park said, waving him away from it. "Now this next item you should find particularly interesting. It was found in New Guinea and as near as I can tell it is in fact one of a kind."

The enchantments on the items in the vault required more specific casting that had to be tailored to each item, requiring him to continuously consult the manuscript he'd brought with him to make sure the spells counteracted them. The process was further slowed by Park's obnoxious need to lecture about each item and the lengths he went to acquire them. Henry did his best to look dutifully impressed rather than disgusted with the depths of his greed and recklessness.

Henry bent over, taking a closer look at the display. Unlike the others there was engraving in a circle around the edge of it that looked very familiar.

"I told you that's nothing," Park said. "Now of you--"

Henry stood and glared at him. "This is where you kept the Vase."

"Is it? I had--"

"It wasn't a question and I'm not an idiot. Why is there a second level of warding where the vase would go?"

Park smiled but Henry could see that he was rattled. "Well, as I said before, some items require several layers of warding in order to make sure they can be displayed safely. Now that I think about it yes, that was the stand I used for the Fury Vase."

Henry stalked towards him. "And why does it need a second level of warding?"

"It's hard to say," Park replied, backing up. Henry reached out and grabbed him by the front of his shirt.

He felt her hand on his shoulder before she even said anything. "Mr. Churchill." Her touch was so hot he could feel it down to the soles of his feet. He gritted his teeth and let go of Park's shirt.

"Thank you, Ms. Saunders," Park smirked. "From what I've been told the Vase has a tendency to still affect those it has influenced even with the Furies contained within."

"And you're just telling me this now?"

Park shrugged. "If I told you every bit of lore and rumor about the Vase and its inhabitants your colleagues would still be here taking notes."

"And if it's true then my people will be in danger even

after they complete the ritual."

Park's lips twitched in a poor attempt to hide a smile. "Like I said, it's just a rumor. But better safe than sorry."

Henry narrowed his eyes. "I'm going to check up on them. Anything else I should let them know?"

"I suppose not. But time is of the essence."

Henry took out his phone and dialed Lexie. It rang until it went to voicemail. He typed out a text and turned back to them. "They aren't answering."

"I'm sure they're quite busy. Shall we continue?"

"Yeah," Henry said. "But if something has happened to them we're going to have a problem. Clear?"

"Crystal," Park smiled without an ounce of worry.

"Don't move," Lexie whispered.

"I'm too terrified to move," Harmony croaked, still sprawled out on the floor.

Lexie backed up, half crawling towards the duffle bag of guns. The three of them looked from Harmony to Lexie and back again, their movements in perfect sync. Martin groaned and they turned around to glare at him. When they saw the urn they raised their heads, spread their wings and let loose a deep howl so loud that she felt it vibrating in her bones. The hallway, which she realized had been nearly silent since Furies materialized, erupted in noise. Not just the distant un-repressed clamor of suburban violence but now a wave rushing towards them.

"What happ--oh fuck me," Martin groaned, trying to push himself up off the ground. As soon as he saw the Fury standing on the other side of the table from him he scrambled backwards. The Fury raised its arm and a long, multi-headed whip formed from the trails of smoke around its hand. It swung the whip around its head and Lexie drew her pistol, firing into it to draw its attention to her before it struck. The bullets passed through it and it turned, curving the whip around and lashing out towards her. Lexie rolled over and it hit the carpet with a sizzle after burning its way through a desk. She drew herself up on one knee and fired at the other two, the bullets passing through them like a dense fog only to reform once again with snarls and growls.

"The spell!" Lexie yelled at the flabbergasted Martin. "Finish the goddamn spell!"

The other Furies had formed weapons as well, a long spiked club for one and a curved scythe for the other. The one with the whip turned towards the door of the room and let out another howl. The commotion on the other side of the door reached another crescendo, this time punctuated with savage pounding at the door. Harmony half-crawled, half-ran to the table wedged under the door handle and pushed against it with one arm while she dragged the bag of guns and ammunition towards her.

"Clip!" Lexie yelled, firing the last of her rounds at the

club-wielding Fury and dissipating it into formless black cloud.

Lexie ejected the spent clip and snatched the one Harmony threw her out of the air and slammed it home. As she chambered a round she saw the scythe-wielder advance on Martin as he crawled toward the table and the wobbling, toppled over urn. He just missed the urn with the tips of his fingers and the Fury swung its blade through the table legs closest to it, shearing through them effortlessly. Martin pushed himself forward, catching it in midair with his other hand and rolling away from the Fury as he began the words of the spell again.

Harmony pulled her pistol from the bag and fired at the Fury with the whip as it closed on her. The Fury reformed quicker this time and cracked its whip towards her. Harmony rolled out of the way and the whip burned through part of the table she'd been leaning against. Martin backed up, reciting the spell as fast as he could as the Fury closest to him stalked forward, scythe raised high. Lexie fired three rounds into it and then three more at the Club-Wielder, backing up until she was against the wall. As the Fury in front of her reformed she fired her last three rounds at the Fury closing on Lexie.

She was about to call for another clip when Martin's voice raised again and she could feel the push of the spell against her and inside her. The Furies, all reformed, stopped and turned to him, roaring in unison as if to drown out his words. He held the urn up over his head, turning the mouth of it to face them as the final words of the spell echoed around the room. It looked for a moment as if the Furies were diving towards Martin but as they got close their forms were pulled apart and turned to red streaked smoke, swirling around the lip of the urn before being dragged inside with a low hollow clap.

"Is that it?" Harmony said, sticking her head up from behind the table she'd been crouched behind.

"I don't know," Lexie said, getting to her feet and holstering her pistol.9

"Martin, you okay?"

"Define okay," he said. "Because if okay is feeling like you've just shat your own puke into your brain then I am the golden god of okay."

"Don't be such a baby," Harmony said, picking up the bag and walking over to him.

"Could a baby do this," he said, holding the Urn out, "becau--" His hand twitched and the Urn wobbled out of his palm and he dropped to his knees, grabbing at it frantically and just barely keeping it from hitting the ground.

"Yeah," Harmony said. "Babies do that all the time."

"Jesus, be careful." Lexie said, reloading her Walther. When the metal snap of the round being chambered echoed in the room she turned towards the door. "Do you hear that?"

"I don't hear anything," Martin said, gathering up the ritual and spell notes that had been scattered all over the floor as he clutched the Urn to his chest.

"Yeah, exactly," Harmony said, leaving the bag and moving with Lexie towards the door.

Lexie waved Harmony back as she approached the door. Lexie kicked the table pinning it closed off to the side and backed up, Walther raised. None of the previous riot from the hallway picked back up and after a moment she crept back up to the door and put her ear to it. Still nothing. She looked over to Harmony and nodded for her to be ready. She turned the knob and the door fell open, propelled by the stack of bodies on the floor piled against it.

"Oh shit," Martin said, coming up behind them. "Did we do that?"

Lexie squatted down and examined them. The hallway was littered with the bodies of the formerly riotous citizens and police, all of which covered in an assortment of bruises, tattered clothes and blood that may or may not have been their own.

"Are they..." Harmony asked as Lexie stood up.

Lexie shook her head. "Unconscious. And let's get out of here while they are so we don't have to answer any stupid questions."

Lexie was able to push her way through the pile of bodies, clearing a path for Martin and Harmony to follow. The piles of affluent suburbanites thinned out the further down the hallway they went but their injuries were more and more severe. Tattered clothes, blood, bruises, and one woman that had half of what used to be an expensive purse sticking out of her mouth. Once they could step without worrying about adding to someone's injuries Lexie reached into her jacket for her phone. "I'll let Henry kn…oh crap."

"What?" Harmony asked.

"Henry called and sent a text tha - -," before she could finish one of the Mendhamites on the ground grabbed her ankle and glared up at her through swollen eyes.

"You don't belong here," he slurred through mouth of chipped teeth.

"Oh what the hell!" Martin cried, jumping back as one of the people near him stirred and took a lazy swing at him.

"We've got to go!" Lexie said, kicking her foot loose. "The Furies are still in their heads!"

All around them the battered bodies began to get to their feet, most shaking their heads and blinking rapidly as if they'd been startled awake from a deep sleep. Those that came to first lunged at the barely conscious ones before they realized what was going on, swinging fists and screaming their unrepressed grievances once again.

"Go, go," Lexie said, waving Martin and Harmony forward while keeping her eyes on the larger sized pile of humanity behind them. In such close quarters it was hard to keep track of exactly what was happening but after a few seconds the throng of humanity began to part as Preston, face red with blood and fury, began clearing a path through them with his baton.

"There! Will! Be! Order!" he screamed. Preston grabbed the hair of a man who was choking a woman at least half his age and separated the two with a series of kicks to the man's arms. The woman lunged forward and Preston sent her flying back with a swing of his baton. Lexie was about to turn away when Preston looked up through the crowd and caught sight of her.

"Don't you fucking move!" he screamed, drawing his pistol.

She crouched down, drawing her Walther again, and ran after Harmony and Martin. They'd almost made it to the front of the building but were blocked by a crowd of brawling citizens that Harmony was trying to clear the way through.

"Get down!" Lexie yelled at them, looking back to see Preston pushing his way through the crowd as he sighted down his pistol at them. Martin grabbed Harmony's shoulder with his free hand and pulled her down as Preston opened fire.

The shots went wild, shattering one of the large panes of glass in the building's facade. The sounds of violence were replaced with screams of panic as self-preservation overrode the Furies spell, sending the masses to the edges of the building, clearing a path for Harmony and Martin to leave. With the crowd thinned Preston and Lexie had a clear line of fire at each other. Preston took aim but she drew and fired three rounds into his chest and stomach. He dropped to the ground and Lexie hoped he'd secured his vest properly.

She pushed her way through the crowd and made it outside. Harmony and Martin had made it across the street and into the car, its engine growling to life. The Mustang lunged out of its spot and swerved in a wide arc, narrowly missing a crowd of panicked people as it came around for Lexie. It just barely came to a stop long enough for her to throw the door open and jump in.

"What the hell was that!" Martin said from the backseat. "I thought the spell was supposed to stop this."

"Henry sent me message that even once the Furies were back in the Urn they could still affect people," Lexie said. "We've got to get back to Park's so Henry can secure it."

"Fantastic," Harmony laughed, pulling away "You know you guys--" she was interrupted by the crack of gun fire. Lexie turned and saw Preston firing at them as he got into one of the cruisers parked in front of the community center.

"Persistent little shit isn't he?" Harmony said, gunning the engine.

"No kidding," Lexie said, taking out her phone. "Just try to lose him. I'll let Henry know we're on our way."

"They're alive, I presume?" Park asked after Henry had ended his call.

"Yeah, they are. And they're on their way here with police close behind. Something that could've been avoided if you'd been straight with us from the beginning."

Park rolled his eyes. "Very well. I'll make some calls, you just see to it that the Urn makes it safely into its containment."

"Of course. Ms. Saunders, would you mind helping me with the pedestal?"

"Certainly," she said with a smile, walking over to the stone pedestal and picking it up. "Where should we take it?"

Henry looked over at Park, who scowled. "The office is fine, Ms. Saunders. Where it used to be."

"Of course, sir." She walked out of the vault and headed for the stairs.

"Strong lady," Henry said. "You certainly were lucky to find her."

Park scowled. "Indeed. Do you require anything else before you finish up, Mr. Churchill?"

"Not a damn thing. But I'm going to head up and keep an eye out for my associates in case they need anything when they arrive."

"Fine," park said to Henry's back as he turned and walked away from him. "I just hope this doesn't go on much longer. I do have other matters to attend to."

By the time Henry made it upstairs Ms. Saunders was in the living room waiting for him. "The display has been set up, Mr. Churchill."

"Great. I believe my friends are on their way back and could use some assistance. Could you join me at the gate?"

"Certainly," she said.

Outside they could hear the sirens and screeching of tires, both getting louder. "You may want to have the gate open for them," Henry said, following her down the driveway.

"It does seem like they are in a bit of a hurry." She gave the barest hint of a smile.

"Thank you," he said, putting a hand on her shoulder. "And I'm sorry."

The faint smile disappeared. "Whatever for?"

"It's nothing," Henry said, but the roar of the Mustang's engine as it crested the top of the driveway nearly drowned it out. It raced past them and came to a stop with a skid.

Martin staggered out of the back seat, clutching the Fury Vase to his chest. "Oh god," he said. "I think I'm going to puke into an urn full of mythology."

"Don't be such a baby," Harmony said, getting out.

"Knock it off," Lexie said. "We still ha--" there was a crash and the rending sound of metal at the bottom of the driveway rang out over the sirens. The police car that had been following them had just barely made it through the closing gate, the edge of it dragging along the back panel of the car and shearing off the bumper.

"Get inside," Henry yelled at them as the cruiser came to a halt and the cop inside tumbled out and into the driveway. His face was smeared with blood and his eyes were bloodshot as he struggled to draw his pistol.

"Not a chance," Lexie said, her own pistol drawn and taking aim at the cop as she put herself in front of Martin and Harmony.

"Sir," Ms. Saunders said. "You are trespassing. I'm afraid I'll have to ask you to leave."

"Lady, get down," Lexie yelled, but Henry waved her off.

"She'll take care of it," Henry said.

"This guy is completely unhinged, Henry," she said, trying to get around him so she could get a clear shot. The cop finally yanked his pistol free and raised it to Ms. Saunders, who had closed to within five feet of him.

"You're under arrest!" he screamed. "You're all under arrest!"

"You need to go," she said, reaching out to him.

He fired directly into her outstretched hand with no effect.

"Come on," Henry said, backing up. "You don't want to see this."

"I don't know," Harmony said. "I kind of…" she trailed off as Ms. Saunders' body began to crackle with sparks like dry kindling. She grabbed the pistol and pulled the cop in close, her other hand grabbing the front of his shirt. "I told you," she said, her body bursting into flame, "you need to go."

"Yeah we need to go," Martin said, turning and darting

inside, arms wrapped around the Urn, the others following close behind.

"So this is what you meant," Lexis said, now out of earshot of the screams.

Henry nodded. "The Saunders estate was nearly burned to the ground when Ellen Saunders had a fainting spell while carrying a lamp back to her bedchamber. She and her whole family were killed."

"Tragic," Park said, waiting for them next to her desk. "But it allowed me to purchase the property for quite a bargain, especially given how many small fires and other...unpleasant incidents the estate had seen over the past hundred years."

"So now she's what, your ghost slave?" Lexie snarled.

"I prefer the term 'assistant.' And clearly a very valuable one, since she was able to clean up after your unfortunate mess."

"I'll give you an unfortunate mess," Harmony said, reaching for her baton.

"Please," Ms. Saunders said, walking briskly back into the room, looking perfectly normal and without any sign she'd been a human bonfire moments ago. "There's no need for further violence. That nasty officer has been removed from the premises."

"Fantastic," Martin said, his face pale. "Can I let go of this now?"

"But of course," Ms. Chalmers nodded, taking it gently from him and walking into Park's study.

"Well," Park said. "There's still some work to be done in the basement. Mr. Churchill?"

"Are you fucking kidding me?" Harmony said. "After you nearly got us killed?"

"It's fine," Henry said. "I'm almost finished. It won't take too much longer." He looked and Lexie and nodded and she nodded back.

***

"So how'd it go down there?" Lexie asked when Henry emerged from the vault a couple of hours later.

"Fine," he said. "Starving and exhausted, but I think I'm going to make it. How's it going up here?"

"Harmony is still pretty pissed but she's behaving herself. Martin crashed out about a half hour ago. I think we may end up having to give him hazard pay. Or business cards that say 'apprentice,' on them."

"Hopefully this will just be a one-time thing. Where's Park?"

"In his office. He kicked us out a little bit ago and said he had work he needed to catch up on."

"Then let's get out of his hair, then." The two walked through the living room, Lexie pausing to shake Martin awake in his chair, and to Ms. Saunders' office.

"We're done," he said. "Can you let him know we're

ready to settle up?"

"Certainly, Mr. Churchill," she said, getting up and opening the door to his office. "They're finished," she said and Park looked up from his computer.

"Excellent," Park said. "All things considered that went quite well. Perhaps we can do this again next year when the wards need strengthening again. Even if the young lady who did them before wanted to return I wouldn't have her back given her apparent inexperience."

"Apparent?" Lexie said. "She broke the Fury Vase."

Park chuckled. "I never said she broke it. The Vase had been part of her original deal but without the supplemental warding it began to degrade. She brought it back here to inquire how to fix it and that's when it finally shattered. She was...displeased."

"I bet," Lexie said. "Jesus, you're just full of little surprises aren't you?"

Park grinned. "I answered all your questions. It's not my fault you didn't ask the right ones. Now, the manuscripts?"

Lexie nodded and took the book they'd gotten from Martin and the one from Mrs. Chalmers out of the duffle bag and set them on Park's desk.

He looked down at them and then back up with a glare. "Only two? There are nineteen volumes."

"And two of them is what we have," Henry said. "Now tell me what you know about her."

"For just two volumes?"

"It's not our fault you didn't ask the right questions," Lexie said. "Now talk. We had a deal."

"I just didn't know it was for only two volumes, that's all," he said, walking over to his desk and taking out a slip of paper. "I'm not entirely sure how to get in touch with her, as she sought me out. But this is her name and the number she gave me." He walked around the desk and then stopped, holding the paper in his hand with a gleam in his eye. "But maybe we should make an arrangement for next year before I hand it over. There aren't that many practitioners in the tri-state area that have your level of skill, Mr. Churchill."

"No, there aren't and no, I won't." Henry said, holding his hand out. "The information, please."

"Mmmm," Park said, pulling the piece of paper away. "Perhaps I can persuade you. Ms. Saunders?"

There was a gust of burning ozone and she knew Saunders was right behind her.

"Are you fucking kidding me?" Lexie said, whirling around and drawing her Walther. Henry raised a hand to her as Ms. Saunders took a step towards her. Lexie nodded, raising her free hand as she reholstered her weapon.

"Ellen," Henry said, drawing her gaze to him. "I know you don't want to do this."

"Are you serious?" Park said. "She's bound to this house and the house is mine. It's a simple thing, Mr. Churchill.

Enter in to a new contract with me and I'll give you what you want."

"I gave you what I want," Henry said, not taking his eyes off Ellen. She was staring at him as if she was trying to place where she had seen him before. "But then you changed the deal. How the hell am I supposed to trust you again?"

"Fine," Park said in annoyance. "I'll give you what you want."

"Yes, you will," Henry said, whispering words to himself and stepping forward to put his hand on Ellen's shoulder. It was as hot as it was when she'd touched him before but this time her eyes went wide and she let out a gasp. "Ellen Saunders," he said. "I release you from this house and from your guilt. What happened was an accident."

Her lip trembled and the flesh under his hand grew warmer. "No, I got scared and I--"

"Ellen," Henry said again. "It was an accident. I release you. Your family is waiting for you."

"What the hell are you doing?" Park said, coming around the desk. Lexie stopped him in his track, hand reaching back for her pistol.

"Taking away an asset," she smirked.

"It's okay," Henry said to her. "It's over now. You can go home. Go home and rest. I release you."

She let out a sigh and closed her eyes as Henry took his hand off her shoulder. "No!" Park yelled as she lost shape, fading into the swirling black mist and vanishing in a cloud of black, acrid smoke.

"Looks like you're hiring," Lexie said, reaching out and snatching the piece of paper from his hand.

Park's mouth gaped open and closed and then he turned to glare at Henry in rage, "How? Do you know how much magic it took for me to bind her spirit to do my will?"

Henry nodded. "A lot, I bet. And it was probably similar to the magic I used when warding your home. Which, by the way, allowed me to exorcise any spirits on the grounds. Come on, we're done here."

"Just one more thing," Lexie said, picking up a marker up from the desk and walked over the Urn. "Real important." She nodded to Henry and he lifted the glass case that now covered the Urn. She leaned down and write on the side of the Urn.

"What are you doing?" Park said, lunging forward, but Harmony put a hand in the center of his chest to stop him.

"Easy slick," she said with a sweet smile. "I've got a taser here that I've been dying to use all day." Before he could protest any more Lexie stood up, capped the marker and tossed it back on the desk.

"There we go, all done, she said. She nodded at Henry and he lowered the glass case down over it. He and Martin walked around to get a closer look.

"Oh man, classic," Martin said.

Written on the side of the urn in bold print was "ONLY DUMB ASSHOLES COLLECT CURSED MAGIC KNICKNACKS" and below that "DO NOT BREAK FURIES INSIDE."

"Both good warnings," Henry said. "Done?"

"Yup," Lexie said, turning and walking out the door.

"I wouldn't feel so smug!" Park shouted after them. "I know why she wanted the Fury Vase. She meant them for you! For both of you!"

They stopped and turned around. "What? Why?" Henry said.

Park nodded, smiling angrily. "Because of what the two of you did to her father."

"Holy shit," Lexie said, pulling out the piece of paper and opening it. Henry took it from her, looking at it and then back up at Park.

"This can't be true," Henry said, but Park just nodded his head furiously.

"It is! Now get the fuck out of my house!"

"Who is it?" Harmony said as they walked quickly out the back door. Henry showed her and looked over at Lexie, whose face was blank as she headed over to Harmony's Mustang.

"Whoa," Harmony said, stopping in her tracks as she read it with Martin reading over her shoulder. "Morgana McCabe? I didn't know Owen had a daughter."

"Me either," Henry said.

The end of "Fall of Shadows"

but Lexie Winston & Henry Churchill will return in

"The Lamentable Catalog"

in the third collection

"Dead of Winter"

ABOUT THE AUTHOR

Thacher E. Cleveland grew up in New Jersey and upstate New York and has lived in Ohio, Chicago, and currently resides in Tennessee with his girlfriend and several cats. He writes a lot of things like novels (SHADOW OF THE PAST), short stories (The Winston and Churchill supernatural private investigator series) and comics (Mythpocalypse), as well as creates dumb stuff for people to buy. Plus he does some acting on the side.

He is very tired. You can find him online at www.demonweasel.com, or on Twitter, Instagram, and Tumblr (@demonweasel), if you're into that kind of thing.

23551208R00155

Made in the USA
Columbia, SC
11 August 2018